Learning Centre

Park Road, Uxbridge Middlesex UB8 1NQ
Renewals: 01895 853326 Enquiries: 01895 853344

Books by Robert Swindells

BRANDED

BROTHER IN THE LAND

DAZ 4 ZOE

DOSH

NO ANGELS

A SERPENT'S TOOTH

SMASH!

STONE COLD

WRECKED

For younger readers

THE ICE PALACE

BRANDED

ROBERT SWINDELLS

PUFFIN

For Alastair Wilbee

PUFFIN BOOKS

Published by the Penguin Group
Penguin Books Ltd, 80 Strand, London WC2R ORL, England
Penguin Group (USA), Inc., 375 Hudson Street, New York, New York 10014, USA
Penguin Books Australia Ltd, 250 Camberwell Road, Camberwell, Victoria 3124, Australia
Penguin Books Canada Ltd, 10 Alcorn Avenue, Toronto, Ontario, Canada M4V 3B2
Penguin Books India (P) Ltd, 11 Community Centre, Panchsheel Park, New Delhi – 110 017, India
Penguin Group (NZ), cnr Airborne and Rosedale Roads, Albany, Auckland 1310, New Zealand
Penguin Books (South Africa) (Pty) Ltd, 24 Sturdee Avenue, Rosebank 2196, South Africa

Penguin Books Ltd, Registered Offices: 80 Strand, London WC2R ORL, England

www.penguin.com

First published 2005
1

Set in 10.5/15.5 pt Linotype Sabon
Typeset by Rowland Phototypesetting Ltd, Bury St Edmunds, Suffolk
Made and printed in England by Clays Ltd, St Ives plc

British Library Cataloguing in Publication Data
A CIP catalogue record for this book is available from the British Library

ISBN 0-141-31728-0

1

By eleven she's had enough, even in the chill-out room. The others'll be here till two or after but she's nauseous, headache on the way. She makes her excuses, gets up to go.

Take care, gorgeous, grins Carl, there's a nutter out there.

Sandra nods. Yeah, take a taxi, Caro: no walking.

No cabs are standing by, it's a bit early. The cold air's clearing her head, she feels better already. Home's a mile, lighted all the way. Even nutters don't strike in full view of passers-by.

She's about halfway when she realizes she should've peed before leaving the club. Nuisance but no great prob: there's a little park coming up, where rhododendrons crowd right up to the railings. She's used it before, they all have. It's a jungle, impenetrable by prying eyes.

Squatting with her jeans round her knees she has no chance. He comes out of the tangle behind her, throws an arm round her throat. Half-throttled, mad with terror, she kicks and writhes and claws at that brawny arm while its owner does to her the things he's driven to do.

You can't do those things and leave your victim alive, unless you want to spend the rest of your life locked up. As his frenzy subsides he flexes the lacerated arm, squeezing, squeezing, till the girl stops kicking and goes limp. He maintains the deadly clamp a full minute to make sure, then lays her like a rag doll on the leaf mould and straightens up, breathing heavily, stooping to knock bits of muck off the knees of his chinos with his hand. Satisfied, he turns and pushes his way through the dark shrubbery, leaving somebody's daughter to be found by a dog in the morning.

2

Hey, Parish, you spacer!

It's ten to nine. I'm walking the furthest margin of the playing field, waiting for the buzzer. I don't like this school or anybody in it, and nobody likes me. I'm out here hoping to be left alone, but no chance. Hawthorne's a predator and I'm his prey: the new boy who talks funny. Here they come, him and his sidekicks, cutting across the middle. Hawthorne, Wilson and Baird: the Market Flaxton Mafia. I wait, no point doing anything else.

You're a nutter, Parish, d'you know that? He calls this from the centre circle, can't wait to get on my case.

I shake my head, call back. I'm as sane as you are, Hawthorne. Saner.

Ha! They approach, surround me. Hawthorne gives me a shove. I don't talk funny, do I? Don't talk to myself like you do.

I don't talk to myself.

Yes, you do, we heard you: isn't that right, lads? The

sidekicks nod. We was by the shed, says Baird, yesterday, having a swift drag. You trogged past saying your name.

Yeah! jeers Wilson. Your *name*: how barmy's that?

I feel myself blush. I can't deny it, I *do* say my name, but only when I think I'm alone.

And what about the weird accent? pursues Hawthorne. I reckon you're one of them asylum seekers.

I shake my head. We're from the north.

North *what*, goes Baird: Pole? They fall about.

Anyway, says Hawthorne when he's managed to control himself, you're some sort of foreigner and nut, and me and the lads think you better go back where you came from, quick-sticks.

I wish I could, I retort. This is the crummiest dump I've ever been in, but my dad's firm transferred him so we're stuck.

It's too good for you, says Wilson. You're a brain-dead tunnel-dwarf and you belong on the council tip.

Yeah, goes Hawthorne, they sent a limo.

They grab me and rush me across the muddy field. I try to dig my heels in but they're three fit guys, I've no chance. We're off to the wheelie bins by the kitchen door. It's not the first time.

The sidekicks hold me while Hawthorne lifts lids and peers in, looking for the messiest one. Custard's best, or gravy or old grey fat. There's always one like that. He finds it and they bundle me in, to cheers from kids who've gathered to watch. The lid comes down and I'm in custard, in the dark. It's a rotten thing to do to a guy, but when you're me you have to remind yourself it could be worse. A lot, lot worse.

3

Min?

What? It's bedlam in the newsroom, they both have to shout.

DP wants a word, his office, now.

Shit! Minnie snatches an e-mail from the printer tray, spikes it and stands up. Danvers Pilkington, Editor-in-Chief of the *Post*, always wants everything now, and if he doesn't get it somebody's job's on the line. Minnie Cooper needs her job. She trots along the corridor.

You wanted a word, DP?

I did. I do. This Ward business.

The relocation?

Yes. I'm damned if I'm going to let 'em slip away, Minnie. You were at the trial, know 'em by sight: I want you to track 'em down.

But, DP, what about the . . .

Gagging order? Listen, I didn't get where I am today by sticking to the letter of the law. This paper, *my* paper, has always upheld the public's right to know. How would you like it if they put the family of a serial killer next door to *you* without letting you know? *Morning, Mrs So-and-So. Beautiful day. Got anything planned have you: nice*

4

strangling, perhaps? Infringement of civil rights, I call that.

Yes, but . . .

No buts, Minnie. You get to work and sniff 'em out, and let *me* worry about the law. The law's an ass and I'm an ass*hole*, and that's a winning combination. If you doubt me, take a look at our circulation stats.

4

What have you *come* as, Parish: you look as though you spent the night in the back of a dustbin wagon. This from Shikey Fenton, my registration teacher. Don't ask me why the kids call him Shikey: I've no idea. What I do know is, he's not my number one fan.

Sorry, sir, I slipped and fell in some muck. I tried to get it off, but . . .

Spare me the life story, lad: get a grip for goodness' sake, try to fit in.

Yessir. I sit down, take a book out of my bag, pretend to read. I can hear Hawthorne and his mates behind me, giggling. I count to ten slowly. My counsellor reckons it helps.

Spare me the life story. I'll do that, Shikey; I'm supposed to forget it myself only I can't. I can't. Fourteen years and none of it ever *happened*? Yeah, right. What's Gav doing at this moment? I wonder.

Know what hell is? Missing someone you love, and

5

I don't mean when they're away on holiday or working abroad: I mean when they're never coming back. I keep seeing Gav, it's weird but my counsellor says it's normal. I'll catch sight of him out of the corner of my eye, walking away or in a crowd. My heart'll kick me in the ribs, I'll double take and hurry after him and it's never him, it's always somebody else. And each time it's like losing him all over again. You gradually come to realize what the word *never* actually means. There's an eternity of desolation in never: ask King Lear.

They called him some terrible names, our Gav. The tabloids I mean. Fiend. Pervert. Beast. Monster. They know nothing about him, it broke Mum's heart.

I'll tell you something about my brother: what he's really like. In our family, when it's your birthday you get to choose what everybody does that day. We're a close family, we like to do things together. Of course it might not be the actual day, because there's work and school: it might have to wait till Saturday. I love theme parks with plenty of white-knuckle rides, so last year, for my thirteenth, I chose Flamingoland. I'd been before, it has seriously scary rides. Trouble was, this particular day turned out to be the wettest since records began. We tried to have a good time but it bucketed down non-stop; you got your bum wet every time you sat on a ride, and it was no fun huddled over fish and chips with puddles round your feet. At half-twelve we packed it in and drove home.

That was in May. Gavin turned eighteen in August. He's into bowling, but he didn't take us bowling this time, he took us to Flamingoland. Reckoned he'd developed an enthusiasm for it, but I knew that wasn't true. Truth is he was doing it for me, because my day'd been a wash-out. That August Saturday was a scorcher and we went on everything. I had the best birthday ever, even though it wasn't mine, and that's the sort of guy my brother is.

You won't read *that* in the paper.

5

Oooh, Gav, what've you done to your arm? This is Mum to my brother, in the bathroom. He's just come from work, he's washing for dinner. She's putting towels in the airing cupboard.

Nothing, Mum. Bad load this morning: razor wire. I got this unloading. Gav drives a truck for a small haulier, gets every kind of load.

Mum sighs. They should pay you danger money for jobs like that, Gav: razor wire. Hang on and I'll get some cream, bandage it up for you.

No, Mum, it's all right.

You don't want it to get infected, love.

It'll be fine, Mum, honestly. Happens all the time.

We never eat till Dad gets back, which varies. Today he's installing domestic alarms out Malton way so it'll be late. I'm in the front room with Kirsty, gawping at the telly. I watch the kiddy shows with her, then it's the news. Another girl's been murdered, some guy walking his dog found the body. Mum doesn't like my sister seeing that stuff, so I tell her there's a choc bar up in my room that's hers if she can find it. There really *is* one: I wouldn't do a dirty trick like that. It's in the drawer of my bedside unit and it's small, so it won't spoil her appetite.

As she leaves the room Gav comes in, ruffles my hair. How's it hanging, bro?

Sssh!

What?

I'm listening, there's been another murder.

Another girl?

Yeah, listen. I turn up the volume. He joins me on the sofa and we watch. Bushes, railings and that blue-and-white tape. A solemn-faced reporter talks to camera.

Hey, I know that place, goes Gav. It's Sparrow Park, I used to play footie there.

I nod, wishing he'd shut up and listen. Caroline Summers, the victim's called. She was eighteen and she's the fifth. Sexually assaulted and strangled like the other four. I know I shouldn't be, but I'm fascinated. I remind myself she was somebody's *kid* once, like our Kirsty. I ought to be horrified, full of sorrow and pity for her family, not glued to it like it's an episode of *Inspector Frost*, but that's how they present it: like it's a soap.

Different story if I'd known I was sharing a sofa with the killer, because we only really feel stuff when it involves *us*, don't we?

6

They arrest him at work when he gets back off a job. It's a Tuesday. I get a message to go to the head's office. He looks at me funny, says I'm wanted at home straight away.

What's happened, sir? I ask, and he says he doesn't know. Out by the bike shed I use my mobile. Dad picks up. What's *he* doing home this time of day?

Dad, what's up?

I . . . not over the phone, son. Come home quick as you can.

Is it Mum?

No, your mum's all right. Just get here, will you?

Pedalling, swerving through traffic, I try to guess. Kirsty's been knocked down: she's critical. Gav's truck's jackknifed: he's dead. Mum and Dad have debts they've kept from us: we've lost the house and everything. I'm adopted: my real parents've come for me. My imagination's in overdrive, but it doesn't come up with anything half as bad as what's actually waiting for me at home.

Dad's in the kitchen; he lays an arm across my shoulders, steers me through to the sitting room. Where's Mum? I ask.

Sit down, son, your mum's upstairs having a rest.

Kirsty?

At school, I'll go fetch her in a minute. Listen. You know the murders: those girls?

Sure, I know.

Well, they're saying it was our Gav.

Who's saying it, are they crazy?

The police. They've arrested him. Your mum's hysterical, I've sent for the doctor.

But it's a mistake, right? A *mistake*. Our Gav . . .

I think so, son, yes. I *hope* so, but I wanted us all together. To be honest I didn't know *what* to do. I want you to listen for the doctor, take him up to your mother while I fetch Kirsty. Will you do that?

Well, yeah, but like, shouldn't one of us be with Gav? He'll be frantic.

There's a solicitor, she's with Gav at the moment. She'll see they don't . . . he's not alone. I better go.

When he's gone I sit on the sofa, staring at the carpet. I can hear Mum crying in her room. I don't know whether to go up to her or wait for the doctor. I'm mad at the police for causing all this with their silly mistake. Because it *is* a mistake, isn't it: *has* to be. Our Gav wouldn't hurt a fly.

But it isn't. Turns out it isn't. They come while the doctor's still here, two detectives. They want to talk to Mum but the doctor doesn't let them, he's given her pills. They search Gav's room and find things he kept, from the girls. I don't know this at the time, just that they've got some stuff in plastic bags. Maybe I should've asked if they had a search warrant but I don't think of it: don't expect 'em to find anything.

Gav, my hero. The guy I want to be like when I grow up.

7

It's amazing how quickly it got impossible. To carry on I mean. To stay. You'd think people'd have the intelligence to realize it isn't the family's fault, but it seems they don't. And, of course, the papers don't help, with their lurid headlines. They stir people up, tell them the public's outraged by what's happened. They're not outraged at all, of course, just interested. It's another soap to them, but if your paper says ordinary decent people're outraged, you better *act* outraged or people might think you're not decent.

Our Kirsty's seven. She had a best friend, Laura Throup. The day after they took my brother into custody, Laura turned up at school with a note for the teacher. When she'd read it, the teacher told Kirsty to get her stuff together and change places with Angela Battersby. From now on Angela was to sit next to Laura, and Kirsty would sit beside Tara Wigglesworth.

When Mum collected my sister at the end of the school day, Kirsty and Laura crossed the yard together as usual. But when they reached the gateway Mrs Throup darted forward, grabbed Laura's arm and hurried her away without so much as a word. Kirsty didn't seem to notice, but told Mum on the way home she wasn't sitting next to her friend any more. As soon as they got in, Mum phoned the school and was told by an embarrassed teacher that

Mrs Throup had written that she didn't want her child contaminated by that monster's sister.

This broke Mum up, coming on top of everything else. Remember, our Gav hadn't even been tried then. And it got worse. Next day Tara's mother collared the teacher to ask why the killer's sister had been put with *her* daughter. Kirsty was moved again, this time on to a little table by herself. *Seven years old*. She didn't know the meaning of the word murder. Mum took her away from school.

It went on like that. A day or two after the trial, a woman slapped Mum's face in Suresave. Marched up to her at the check-out, fetched her a terrific slap and stalked off without a word. She might've been related to one of the girls, but I doubt it. Probably just being ordinary, decent people.

The trial had knocked all the stuffing out of Mum. She hadn't the will to retaliate, or even protest. She stood with one hand covering her bruised cheek, crying quietly till a security guard came and steered her outside. It wasn't till she was on the car park with her empty shopping bag that she realized he hadn't been rendering assistance: Suresave no longer required her custom.

They must have known. That's what people were saying about us. Gavin couldn't possibly have murdered five women and hidden odds and ends of their property in his room without the rest of us knowing what was going on.

What did they think used to happen? Did they think we saw Gav come home with blood on his jeans and somebody's phone in his hand and go, *Oh-oh, looks like our Gav's been at it again, the rascal. Shame he can't get interested in bird-watching or collecting stamps, but still . . .*

We knew nothing, that's the truth. How many parents know what a eighteen-year-old has in his room? As far as we were concerned, Gav drove a truck for a haulage firm and went bowling with his mates in his spare time. He didn't even have a girlfriend. And if there was ever blood on his jeans he didn't flaunt it.

Some local folk even turned up one Saturday morning to harass us at home. Dad worked till lunchtime Saturdays, but Mum was in. I happened to glance out the window at about ten and there they were, eight of them. Two had placards, one with PERVERTS OUT in felt-tip. I couldn't read the other.

I told Mum we should call the police. She said, D'you think the police'll come rushing to protect us, Dale? *Us?*

I punched in three nines anyway, asked for the police. A woman's voice said, How can we help? I said, There's a mob outside our house, I think they're going to attack.

May I have your name, please?

Ward. Dale Ward.

And the address?

Nine Ranelagh Drive. Can you hurry please: my dad's at work and I'm here with my mother and sister, she's only seven.

These people: what're they doing exactly?

Standing by our gate, looking at the house.

That isn't an offence, you know. They're not throwing stones or anything like that: causing damage?

Not so far, but I can tell they haven't come to see if we want any shopping done.

All right, Dale, we've a car in the area. Should be there in a minute or two.

Thanks a lot. Bye.

They're sending a car, Mum.

Thank goodness. Call Dad will you, love, let him know what's happening?

Dad, it's Dale. There's a bunch of people outside the house, we've called the police.

What people, son? What're they doing?

Nothing yet. It'll probably be OK, a police car's coming.

Good. Lock both doors; keep Kirsty away from windows. I'll be there in ten minutes.

There's no need, Dad, they'll run a mile when they see the car.

I . . . I was coming anyway, Dale. He hung up.

I went through to the kitchen. Dad's coming.

Oh dear, perhaps we shouldn't have bothered him at work. They've been so good to him about . . . you know?

He said he was coming anyway.

Did he? That's strange, this early. Go see what those idiots're doing, I hope they don't set about your dad.

Police'll be here by then, Mum.

I hope so, Dale.

The patrol car drew up opposite just as I looked out. There was no siren or flasher but it did wonders. The heroes shuffled about for a minute looking uncomfortable, then began to disperse. The coppers didn't even have to say anything. By the time Dad's van appeared they'd all gone. The patrol car moved off. Dad came up the path.

Everybody all right? he said in the kitchen doorway.

Mum nodded. What about yourself, David: are *you* all right?

He shrugged, pulled a face. They've given me the push, he said.

8

There's this movie, *Being John Malkovich*. Guy finds a little door behind a filing cabinet, turns out to be a way into John Malkovich's head: a portal. You crawl through and *become* the famous actor for a while. Weird.

I'm being Glen Parish, and it's doing my head in. I mean, I've been given a new identity. We've all been given new identities, except Gav. We're the Parishes. It's a fresh start for us. I'm supposed to be Glen Parish but I'm not: I'm *being* Glen Parish, which isn't the same. Officially and in theory Dale Ward no longer exists, but try telling my brain cells that. As far as they're concerned I'm Dale Ward: always was, always will be. If somebody yelled Dale I'd turn round. If they yelled Glen I might not, and if I did I'd just be acting, playing a part. *Being* Glen Parish.

It must be a bit like this for a woman who marries and takes her husband's name. Except it wouldn't matter if she forgot one time, signed her old name. There are no hack reporters looking for her: her little slip won't lead to a screaming headline. UNMASKED! MISS ROBIN-SON FOUND LIVING AS MRS JONES. Makes a big difference.

My parents keep their first names, and that's *all* they keep. Mum was a librarian, fully qualified. Now she's behind the counter in a tourist-information centre. Half her old salary but better paid than Dad, who's a security guard. Back home he was a security-systems engineer, making good money. Anna and David are still Anna and David, but they're *being* Mr and Mrs Parish, looking over their shoulders for those hacks, watching every word as they scrimp and save and cry over their first kid, locked away forever. So, yes, a fresh start, but there's no place like home, no future like the past.

9

Shikey says, GCSE next year, playtime's over. He holds up a book. *Wuthering Heights*. Who wrote this, anybody know? He's got his hand over the author's name.

I could tell him, but I'm not going to. Why? Because Emily Brontë and her sex-starved sisters are very big where I used to live. Where *Dale Ward* used to live. Wouldn't do for Shikey to start wondering why the new boy knows so much about *Wuthering Heights*. Can't be too careful, see?

Come *on*. He taps the book, cuts his eyes from face to

blanked-out face. Nothing. Not a flicker. He gives us a few more seconds then he's like, Well: by the end of term you're going to know this book and its author inside out. *Inside out*. He uncovers Emily's name. What does it say, Wilson?

Emily Brontë, sir.

Shikey nods. Emily Brontë, late of Haworth, Yorkshire. *Wuthering Heights* was her only novel, and we're going to study it as though it were our set text for GCSE. It's what's known as a *dry run*: a rehearsal for the real thing next year.

Sir? Sally Prentice has her hand up. She's gorgeous, really fit. I could . . .

What is it, Sally? Girls get their first names at MF High, boys don't.

What does it mean, sir?

What does what mean?

Wuthering, sir.

Ah yes: *wuthering*. I understand it's a colloquial term, Sally, referring to the weather. Cold and windy, something like that. And *Heights* refers to the Yorkshire moors.

Oh.

Don't worry, you'll know all about it soon enough. He smiles, rubs his bony hands together. Know why? Because we're *going* there, to Haworth, end of term.

Going there, sir? This from Sally's friend Carla, who isn't bad either. To *Yorkshire*? It's hundreds of miles away, isn't it?

Shikey nods. Yes, but we won't be going on *foot*, Carla. There'll be a coach. A luxury coach that'll whisk us from here to there before you know it. I'm preparing a letter to parents.

My fists're so tightly clenched the nails dig into my palms. *I'm* not going, how can I? We're as well known as Emily Brontë in those parts. What if somebody saw me, recognized me? I can't go, but I'll have to act normal, bring the deposit or whatever, then call in sick at the last minute.

Why *Wuthering Heights*? Why couldn't Shikey have chosen *Great Expectations* or *Moby Dick* or *Far From the Madding Crowd*?

Just my flipping luck.

10

Will Tomlinson's bike's next to mine. He comes up as I'm getting my lock off. Straight home is it?

Yeah. Will's the only kid in school who bothers with me. He's got no mates; he's into archaeology.

Ride along with you?

Be my guest.

We swing through the gateway and freewheel two abreast down Tanner Hill. It's late September, a cool, cloudy afternoon, the sea leaden in the distance.

Will glances at me. Clocked you staring at Sally Prentice.

So? Everyone looks at Sally.

I don't.

You must be gay then. I'm taking a chance winding up my one friend, but hell, even *I*'m entitled to relax now and then.

He chuckles. Better things to do, that's all. Have you seen the dolmen on Hangingwood Down?

Dolmen: what're they?

It isn't a *they*, it's an *it*. Neolithic burial mound.

Ah, no: bit too exciting for me.

It's beautiful, he says, ignoring my sarcasm. We turn left on the Military Road, start pedalling. Great boulders, he continues, you wonder how they even moved them. Balanced on top of one another like they've been stacked any old how, yet inside's dry as a bone: completely waterproof.

No shit.

Thousand years older than the pyramids.

Wow.

I'll be up there Saturday with the digicam, you could come. Bring a sarnie, bottle of water. What d'you say?

I shake my head. Thrill'd probably kill me, Will. Besides, I've stuff to do at home. It's a lie: I've stuff *all* to do, at home or anywhere else, but come on . . . *burial mounds*.

Good day at school, love? asks Mum as I walk in the kitchen. She tries to keep it light, we all do, but we're edgy. Have we kept it one more day, our secret? Shall we sleep tonight, or burn?

I drop my bag, sigh. Does *anybody* have good days at school, Mum?

She shrugs. I think you *used* to, so did Kir– Kayleigh, back at home. She wet the bed again last night, cried all the way to school this morning.

I nod. I'm not surprised: it's doing *my* head in and I'm fourteen. D'you think we'll ever get used to it, Mum?

I'll never get used to having our Gav in *that* place, Glen. Talking through glass, never touching. As for the rest of it, I don't know. It's get used to it or go barmy, as far as I can see.

To cheer her up I tell her about Will Tomlinson, his invitation. *Go*, love, she says. Give him a ring, tell him you've changed your mind.

Serves me right, I suppose.

11

To please Mum I fix it with Will. Today's Thursday, so that's the day after tomorrow sorted. Time to bring up Haworth.

Mum? She's cooking spaghetti: Dad's on nights this week, needs something substantial.

What is it, Glen? Is it on for Saturday?

Yeah, it's on. I wonder if they give out T-shirts: *I rode the dolmen on Hangingwood Down*.

She chuckles, which is rare.

I pull a face. There's a problem.

What, about Saturday?

No, end of term. Shikey's organized a trip, you'll never guess where.

Go on.

Haworth.

Haworth? It's three hundred miles, what's he want to go there for?

Field trip. We're doing *Wuthering Heights*, dry run for GCSE.

Ah.

But *I* can't go, Mum, can I? It's practically on our old doorstep. What if somebody yells *Hey, Dale!* across the street?

Hmm. She lifts the pan off the gas, dumps spaghetti in the colander. I don't know, love. There's certainly a risk, but on the other hand you'd draw attention to yourself by opting out. Let's see what your father thinks.

Dad comes down as David Parish the security guard, wearing the uniform and everything. On his shoulders rides my sister in her role as Kayleigh Parish. He swings her down on to her chair and seats himself. Mum dishes up. We eat.

Between the pasta and the stewed pears, I tell Dad about Shikey's trip. He groans. Why *there*, of all places?

I nod. That's what *I* said. D'you think I should go?

Not really, son. I mean, it'd be daft, wouldn't it, us going through all this hassle, changing our name, moving to the other end of the country, only to have you go back up there and be recognized by some hungry-eyed busybody? No, I think you'll have to chuck a sickie or something when the time comes, Glen. It's a few weeks yet. He shakes his head.

December: who the heck'd want to be on the Yorkshire moors in December if they didn't have to be?

After dinner I go up to my room. I mean to see what I can find on the net about *Wuthering Heights*, but I can't get Sally Prentice out of my head and that's scary, because some of my thoughts are not ones I'd be happy for Mum to read. I won't go into detail because it's embarrassing, but I'm speculating about aspects of Sally that're pretty intimate and none of my damn business, and I don't think a *normal* kid'd be doing that, know what I'm saying? *Am* I normal, that's the point, or am I taking after my brother? Stuff runs in families doesn't it? Have I got what Gav's got, growing inside me?

Will I be a monster?

12

They said he was sane, our Gav. The prosecution put up some psychologist or psychiatrist to say he'd examined my brother thoroughly and there was no doubting his sanity.

I couldn't get my head round that. Still can't. Does it mean a guy can want to do horrific stuff to helpless strangers: want it so badly he can't stop himself doing it, and yet he's got the same sort of mind we've *all* got? If that's the case, how come *everybody* doesn't get those urges? We should be up to here in mutilated bodies, right?

The reason I'm banging on about this is, it's important.

Once there was no doubt Gav had done the things he'd done, we were left clinging to one hope: that he was insane when he did them. If he was he'd be sent to a secure hospital, not prison. Don't get me wrong: a secure hospital *is* a prison. Our Gav'd be locked up in some grim nineteenth-century asylum till he died, but at least there'd be treatment. He'd be a *patient*, not a prisoner. Mum'd be able to tell herself her boy couldn't help it. It was the one pathetic glimmer in her blackness, and that guy blew it out.

The prison's on the Isle of Wight. It was a two-day job for Mum to visit from where we lived before, it's a bit easier from here. She goes whenever he can get a visiting order, takes him stuff like soap, shaving gel, disposable razors. She takes choc bars and orange squash too, and stamps so he'll write to her. Dad's been once, me and Kayleigh haven't. We can't face it, not yet.

It's dangerous, Mum going there: far more dangerous than me going to Haworth. We haven't sussed this, and we won't till it's too late.

13

Minnie Cooper knocks on the door of seven Ranelagh Drive. A woman in jeans and T-shirt opens it a crack. We're Catholics, she says round the cigarette bobbing between her lips, and I never buy at the door.

Mrs Daynes?

Who wants to know?

My name's Minnie Cooper, I write for the *Post*.

Oh. The crack widens a bit. I thought you were one of them Jehovah's Witnesses, or double glazing. What can I do for you?

I'd like to ask you a couple of questions about the people next door, Mrs Daynes. Number nine.

The woman shakes her head. Ash drifts down, settles on the front of the T-shirt. Nine's empty: they did a flit.

I know that, Mrs Daynes. Look, d'you think I could come in for a minute: this drizzle might not look much, but it's starting to come through my jacket.

Oh, yes, of course, sorry. Come in. Would you like a cup of tea?

Only if you take that fag out of your mouth while you're making it, she thinks but doesn't say. She smiles. That'll be lovely, thanks.

She sits on a brown-and-orange sofa upholstered in that shaggy material Yorkshire Terriers seem to be made of. The tea arrives. Minnie checks the surface of hers for ash. Finding none, she sips. Mrs Daynes settles into an armchair and looks across expectantly.

Must've been a bit of a shock, says Minnie, finding you'd got a killer next door?

Well, yes, but of course by the time we found out, he wasn't there: they'd taken him away.

Minnie nods. Of course. Did you know the Wards well, Mrs Daynes: pass the time of day and so on?

Mrs Daynes shakes her head. Not really, no. To be

perfectly honest, I always thought there was something funny about them. I used to say to Mike, that's my husband, there's something funny about that family, Mike.

Really? In what way funny, Mrs Daynes?

I don't know, just funny in general I suppose. He never brought lasses home for one thing.

Who, Gavin?

Yes. Lorry driver, not bad looking, never brought lasses home. Struck me as unusual, that did.

Yes, I see, says Minnie politely. The woman's hindsighted intuitions about her former neighbours are of no interest. In cases of this sort, neighbours can usually be depended upon to imagine they've always sensed something not quite right. She smiles. What I need to know though, Mrs Daynes: what my *paper* needs to know, is where've they gone? Who's got them as next-door neighbours *now*, without knowing it?

Oooh, yes! The woman shivers. I'm glad it's not us any more, I can tell you.

Well, exactly. It isn't fair, and my paper's determined to find out where they're hiding and flush them out. The public has a right to know where they're living, people of that sort. So what I wanted to ask you is this: have you any idea where the Wards might have chosen to go? Did Mrs Ward ever mention a favourite spot, a holiday place perhaps? Did you ever get a postcard? Have a think, Mrs Daynes. It's important.

14

Saturday morning promises to be fine once the sea fret burns off. I get the bike out and stow my lunch box and water bottle in the pannier. If somebody had told me six months ago that I'd pedal four miles uphill to gawp at a Neolithic burial chamber, I'd have said he was barmy. But of course *everything*'s changed in those six months: I don't suppose I'd have crossed the road with a nerd like Will Tomlinson back in the old life.

I pop my head round the kitchen door. Mum's clearing the breakfast things, Kayleigh's helping. I'm off then, Mum.

Got your sandwiches, love, your rain-cape?

I've got everything, thanks.

Good. She smiles briefly. Be careful, and have a good day.

Where you going? asks Kayleigh. Can *I* come?

I pull a face. You'd hate it, sweetheart: it's just some old stones.

I *wouldn't*, I want to come with you.

I shake my head. You'd be bored stiff. She wouldn't: I always wanted to go with our Gav, it didn't matter where. He used to take me sometimes too, in the truck. A bike's not a truck though, I can't possibly take her. I say bye and withdraw my head.

I've looked at an OS map, I know the way. There's not

much traffic, this time on a Saturday. It's mostly uphill, but we're used to hills where I come from. I make good time. By the time I spot the brown *Ancient Monument* sign and hang a right up a steep stony track, the fret's dispersed and the sun's warming my back through the thin T-shirt.

I'm not sure I'll recognize the burial chamber, but I don't have to: Will's there before me. I see him when I'm only halfway up, silhouetted against the pale sky beside a pile of boulders. Nearing the top I see I needn't have worried: the pile of boulders isn't just a pile, it's unmistakably a construction, with a top and sides and a dark, yawning mouth like a cave. I lay the bike beside his on the rabbit-cropped grass and straighten, wiping my brow with my hand.

Will grins. You made it then.

I nod. Yeah, bit winded though.

He nods. They picked the most inconvenient sites for their chambers; nobody's ever really worked out how they got the stones up.

Well, I'm glad they weren't relying on *me*.

He laughs. Me too. I took a couple of shots while I was waiting, look.

We stand with our backs to the sun so the pics show up sharp on the little screen. They're OK, but I can't think of much to say about them. They look fine, I tell him. What d'you do with the printouts?

I've got an album, he says. There are seventeen dolmens in the county, I've visited them all. Some aren't really worth snapping but I've got pics of them, even the collapsed ones and those that've been used as quarries.

Quarries?

Oh, yes. It's only recently people've realized how marvellous these things are, how important it is to preserve them. Before, if somebody wanted stone for a wall or a building they just used to dismantle the nearest dolmen, split the boulders, cart the stone away. There were probably hundreds of them originally, but many will have been totally destroyed.

Oh, right. He seems quite worked up about it. I suppose I ought to fake indignation but I can't. There's a limit to the amount of pretending you can do, my whole life's a fake. *Oh*'s the best I can manage.

He either doesn't notice, or doesn't hold it against me. He shows me how to operate the digicam, then gets me to snap him standing at various points round the dolmen, he says to show scale. Once that's done he lightens up a bit and we start to horse around, snapping each other emerging from the chamber with clawed hands and hideous facial expressions, or launching ourselves off the top. He's actually quite a normal guy under all the archaeology stuff; we have a bit of fun. It isn't till we're sitting with our backs against the boulders, eating our sandwiches that the day gets spoilt for me.

D'you know what's awesome? he says, through a mouthful of banana and peanut-butter sandwich.

What?

How long people're dead, compared with how long they're alive.

I don't know what you mean.

Well, take the people who were buried in this dolmen. They'd live – oh, say forty years. Fifty at the most, and they'd been lying here dead for three thousand years when the *pyramids* were built. That's three thousand years ago, so if they hadn't been disturbed they'd have been here six thousand years by now, and that'd only be the beginning.

Right. It *is* awesome of course, but *right*'s the best I can do, because the mention of dead bodies has given me a fresh angle on the five women Gav murdered. I thought I'd thought everything it was possible to think about them, but I hadn't thought *this* one: that they'd lived about twenty years apiece, and would be dead for six thousand, sixty thousand, sixty *million* years. That's how long my brother's crime would reverberate. That long, and much, much longer.

Didn't do much for my appetite, I can tell you.

15

The sun feels quite hot by the time we finish lunch. We bag the leftovers and put them away so the wasps will leave. I assume *we*'re about to leave too, but Will lies down on the grass and closes his eyes murmuring, This is the life.

I consider going without him but decide against. As I've said, he's not all that nerdy once you get to know him, and besides it looks such a relaxing thing to do, lying in the middle of nowhere with the sun on your face and only the background drone of insects to break the silence. Maybe up here in the pure light of day my mind'll find the peace it never finds at night. After all, somebody slept here for 3,000 years undisturbed.

I do sleep, and the next thing I know Will Tomlinson's got a fistful of my T-shirt and he's shaking me. Glen, he's hissing, wake up, you're having a nightmare.

Glen? goes my fuddled brain, who the heck's . . . oh yeah. I open my eyes, Will's worried face eclipses the sun. 'S OK, I mumble. I'm awake.

He stops shaking, lets go. You were yelling, he says. I thought I better wake you.

Why . . . what was I yelling?

Oh, nothing bad, just noises. Screams. He grins. Probably the stuff we were doing before, you know: playing zombies and that.

Yeah, that's it. I sit up, rake fingers through my hair. It *was* zombies. Thanks for waking me.

You're welcome. Drink?

Oh yeah, thanks. It's his bottle, Strathmore. I drink, he watches me. I won't tell him my nightmare, I daren't.

It wasn't zombies, it was Sally Prentice, in woods somewhere. Dark woods. I only wanted to be close to her, but she wouldn't, she kept running. Then she fell, and when I got to the place she was on the ground with her clothes torn. I looked up and saw the eight people who'd gathered outside our house the day Dad got the sack. I could tell they thought I'd done something bad to Sally. I started to protest my innocence but they took no notice, closing in.

I tried to run but my legs wouldn't obey me. I turned to appeal to Sally and she'd gone, there was just her phone on the ground. They grabbed me and started dragging me towards a dolmen they'd constructed under the trees. None of them spoke, but I knew they'd seal me in blackness for 6,000 years. I began to scream . . .

They say a trouble shared is a trouble halved, but when you're me it pays to keep your troubles to yourself.

16

Market Flaxton must have its own bush telegraph or something. I haven't got the lock on the bike Monday morning before the Mafia pays me a call.

Fun was it, Parish? goes Hawthorne.

What?

Saturday.

It was all right.

Lara there and everything?

Lara?

Croft. You *were* playing Tomb Raider weren't you, you and the Willie?

Oh, *ha*-flippin'-*ha*: you're nearly as funny as a dental abscess, Hawthorne.

We don't *do* funny, Parish. Big mate of the Willie's now then, eh? Sleeping with him?

Don't be stupid.

What then? Don't say you're actually into bleat'n *dolmens*. Nobody's into stuff like that if they've got a life. He turns to Wilson. You into dolmens at all, Nige?

Not so you'd notice, Den.

You, Kim?

Fog off.

See? He looks me in the eye. Know what *I* reckon, Parish?

No, and I don't give a stuff.

I reckon you're sick, sick in the head. That's why you wander round the field muttering your name. Why you go poking about in old graves with losers like the Willie. You're one of them whatsits aren't you: cyclepaths.

What happens next is scary. That he's got the wrong word is irrelevant: he says it to the wrong guy at the wrong time, *that*'s what does it. The bike lock's in my hand and I go for him with it, beating him about the head and shoulders with the springy cable, the metal end. He covers up and backs off but I follow, flailing wildly, battering his wrists and knuckles till the blood spatters the front of his shirt and mine. I'm screeching through bared teeth, can't believe it's me I'm hearing. The side-kicks look on, paralysed. I want their leader dead. *Dead*.

I'm on the way to getting what I want when Royd intervenes. Emma, the kids call her, though her name's Tracey. She's girls' PE. I don't know she's there till a steely arm clamps my neck. Thinking it's Baird or Wilson, I drive my elbow into what I hope's a flabby stomach. Instead of sinking in it bounces off and she squeezes my Adam's apple, going for cider. I'm choking. I grey-out for a second or two, and when my head clears I'm on the ground. Emma squats beside me looking concerned.

17

It's nothing. I'm on my feet in two minutes, one arm round Royd's shoulders. My throat hurts when I swallow, that's all.

Hawthorne's worse, bent over nursing his hands, muttering, He's a nutter, all I said was . . . The sidekicks are attentive, now that they're in no danger. Half the school escorts us across the yard.

She helps me to the first-aid room; insists on it. It's poky: a converted stockroom with a cabinet, some canvas chairs and a foldaway bed. Royd sends Baird and Wilson packing, me and Hawthorne sit side by side while she checks the damage.

You're fine, she tells me and I am, as far as she can see. The blood on my shirt belongs to Hawthorne, it's my mind that's messed up. *Cyclepath*. *Nutter*. Casual diagnoses that reinforce besetting doubts. Hawthorne wasn't to know, of course, he was just unlucky.

His hands're a mess: knuckles skinned and swollen, bruises coming out. There are marks on his face as well, and an angry-looking welt across his forehead. I don't feel proud of my handiwork, and his folks aren't going to be best pleased either: I better hope they won't involve the police, 'cause that'll blow our cover for sure. Royd dabs him with antiseptic, dresses a cut or two, tells him nothing needs stitching.

He'll need stitching, he mutters, looking sidelong at me.

She tells him, That's quite enough. But I'll gladly settle for a vengeful doing if it means no cops.

Tuesday we're hauled up before the head, separately. Waggy's his nickname, for Wagstaff. He gazes at me across a desk the size of a car park. He's got my bike lock on his mouse mat.

You've made an undistinguished start at Market Flaxton High, Parish, he purrs.

I can't very well deny it, standing there with another student's blood on my shirt and the weapon that spilled it between us. Yes, sir, I murmur.

Yes, sir. He sighs. There've been comments from members of staff about the state of your hair, your shoes, your uniform. I'm told you offer no spoken contribution in the classroom, and seem to prefer your own company outside it. And now this. He picks up the lock. Hawthorne tells me you launched an unprovoked attack and beat him savagely. Ms Royd describes your assault as frenzied: apparently she was obliged physically to restrain you.

Not unprovoked, sir, I protest. Hawthorne and his mates were getting at me, they're always getting at me, I retaliated.

You retaliated. Waggy wags the lock, watching its springy movement. How exactly was Hawthorne *getting at* you, Parish? Was he hitting you?

34

No, sir.

What then?

He was winding me up, sir, laughing about where I went on Saturday.

He was winding you up, so you decided to thrash him to within an inch of his life?

I didn't *decide*, sir, it came over me. The lock was in my hand.

He gazes at me. Are you telling me you didn't know what you were doing?

No, I'm not, sir. I knew, I just didn't think.

He nods. Bit excessive, don't you think?

Yes, sir.

Yes, sir. His expression is more shrewd than I like. Well Parish, he says, for all I know your past career may be littered with incidents of this sort, the records from your last school being, shall we say, somewhat incomplete.

It's *not*, sir, I blurt. I've never . . .

I'm glad to hear it, lad. He looks me straight in the eye. Everybody's entitled to a fresh start, Parish, I'm a great believer in that. Your family's moving south con-stitutes a fresh start for you, and it's up to you to make full use of the opportunity. He pulls a rueful face. I know it isn't easy fitting into a schoolful of strangers, especially when some of them are inclined to be ah . . . unhelpful, but here you are, and you might as well buckle down to it. I've spoken to Hawthorne's parents, and fortunately for you they're content to view yesterday's incident as a matter for the school, not the police, so the consequences for you aren't nearly as bad as they might have been. He

35

clears his throat. You will forfeit all privileges for one month, but if anything remotely like this happens again you won't get off so lightly. Understand?

Yes, sir.

18

I sit in biology, weightless with relief. No police, no exposure, no midnight flit that's all my fault. Privileges, forfeiture of. For the first time since they came for Gav, I feel lucky.

These are the privileges I lose for battering Hawthorne:

- Access to the IT suite at lunchtimes and after school.
- Use of the sports centre/equipment at lunchtimes and after school.
- Coming to school out of uniform on Fridays.

Doddle.

Have to watch it though. I'm not daft enough to think the Mafia's going to lay off me from now on. In fact it'll probably be worse, but I can't let it get to me. *Are you telling me you didn't know what you were doing?* How come Waggy lands smack on my pet hang-up: the fear that I might not always be able to control what I do? It's like he knows who I am: whose *brother* I am. He can't though, wouldn't have me in his precious school.

Anyway I'll show him: show *myself*. They can wind me up all they like, I won't lose it again.

Parish! Old Spinal's been banging on about the circulatory system and I haven't heard a word.

Miss?

Tell us what the straw-coloured component of the blood is called, please.

Say lager, hisses a voice behind me.

I . . . sorry, Miss, I don't know.

But I *told* you less than a minute ago, Parish.

Say piss, suggests the same voice. My lips twitch. The briefest of smiles, I can't help it.

Spinal narrows her eyes. I'm glad you find this amusing, Parish: you'll need that sense of humour when you see the GCSE paper. It may seem a long way off now but it creeps up, believe me. *Plasma*'s the word you failed to hear. One of them, anyway.

Thank you, Miss. Her name's Collum, hence Spinal. Kids're tittering all round. I close my eyes, breathe in slowly and think about dolphins.

19

The yard, lunchtime. It's dry and warm. I don't feel deprived: who'd want to be gawping at a screen on a day like this? Better, no one's bothering me: in fact a guy grinned at me just now by the science block. For me, that counts as being lionized.

I know why, of course. I've taken on the Mafia, Hawthorne and his mates're licking their wounds, guys aren't having to watch their backs every minute. Today I'm Beckham, Spider-Man, the Hulk. And, of course, I've always been devastatingly handsome: bit of a chick-magnet in fact. So I'll try my luck, why not?

Sally Prentice and Carla Moffat are sitting side by side on a bench under the staffroom window. It's a plum site, this bench. Nobody's going to hassle you in full view of the teachers, and if you're that sort of creep you can even let 'em see you swotting in your own time. Sally and Carla aren't creeps, they're sharing a fan-mag. I saunter over.

Rate *Club Together*, do you? Club Together's a boy band, Irish, the mag's dedicated to them.

The girls look up, squinting in the sun. They're all right, says Carla, swiping a curtain of blonde hair from her eyes with her hand.

Better than *you*, adds Sally, so it's not a promising start, but I ignore the signs, which shows what a dick I am.

Talking of clubbing together, d'you actually *do* it? Cool line, but it fails to impress.

Do *what*? frowns Sally.

Club together. You know: go clubbing?

What's it got to do with *you*? asks Carla.

I shrug. Thought we might go together sometime, y'know?

What, make up a foursome you mean: me and Sally, you and the *Willie*? She nudges her friend and the two of them just about collapse laughing, they have to prop each other up to stay on the bench. Their whoops attract attention, kids're looking. Shikey Fenton's standing at the window with his hands in his pockets, looking amused.

I should walk away: say something cutting and go. Instead, I dither while my cheeks burn and Beckham, Spider-Man and the Hulk head for the horizon. I rummage through the mess in my mind, desperately seeking words that'll crush these giggling slappers and let me leave with my head up, but there's nothing, and I slink away in front of a yardful of witnesses.

It's a bad moment, and there's something worse. My mind's blanking it but it's there all right, deep down where the slythy toves gyre. I don't want to acknowledge it even to myself, but looking at my tormentors just now I fantasized a way to stop their whooping once and for all. I wouldn't *do* it, of course I wouldn't: everybody has thoughts like that sometimes, it's normal.

Isn't it?

20

Halfway down Tanner Hill, Will grins at me. Just think: if Waggy hadn't stopped your privileges, you might have been punting a ball about in the sports centre at lunchtime instead of making progress with your bird.

Bird?

Sally.

Huh: *what* progress, you corpuscle?

The grin widens. I *saw* you, you had her and Carla laughing like loonies on that bench, couldn't get enough of you.

I shake my head. They were laughing *at* me, mate, not *with* me.

Why, what'd you done?

I pull a face. Not a lot, just asked if they went clubbing.

They do. Young teens night, Hangovers.

Yeah well, I mentioned going with them sometime. That's what cracked 'em up.

Ah. He looks glum. Sorry, Glen, mate: from a distance it looked like you were in there.

Nah, I wish.

We hang a left and he says, I know how you feel, I get the same treatment, and not just from those two. Know what they call me?

I nod. The Willie.

Great, eh? He smiles ruefully. I ignore 'em, get on with my life. Only way.

Yeah.

We ride without speaking for a bit, then he goes, Glen?

Yeah?

Did you have mates at your last school?

Course. I don't expand, hope he'll drop the subject, but he doesn't.

Where *was* it, your last school?

North.

I know that but *where*? He grins. North's a big area.

Jeez, can't he *hear* my reluctance, what's up with him? I shake my head. I don't want to talk about it, Will, all right: it screws me up.

Ah. He nods. Homesick, yeah?

Something like that.

Well, if ever . . . y'know . . . you *want* to talk, I'm here. I mean, *everybody* needs someone to talk to sometimes, right? And it wouldn't go any further. He pulls a face. Who'd listen to the Willie, eh?

I don't respond. He's a sad droop and I feel sorry for him, but he has to understand my history's out of bounds. My *see you* when we separate is deliberately cool. I feel mean but the family's got to come first, and he'd probably be the first to turn on me if he found out who we were.

Look at my mates in the north.

21

Afternoon.

Oh, hello. Want to cross? The old lady brandishes her lollipop, scowls right and left along the road.

Minnie Cooper shakes her head. No, I'm not crossing, but perhaps you can help me another way.

What way? I can't leave here, they'll be out in a minute.

The journalist smiles. I wouldn't ask you to desert your post, Mrs . . . er . . .?

Sugden. Mrs Sugden.

Mrs Sugden. I'm making inquiries about a boy who used to be a pupil here, a Dale Ward.

Oh *him*. Everybody knows about him, *and* that brother of his. Saw the pair of 'em safely across this road hundreds of times, I did. She snorts. I'd've left that Gavin in the middle if I'd known, tanker coming.

Minnie nods. And saved five young women's lives, but you weren't to know, Mrs Sugden: we can't see the future.

No, worse luck.

Minnie smiles. We can *think* about the future though: the future of the victims' families. I work for an organization called MOVE ON, which exists to offer these bereaved families the help they need to put tragedy behind them and move on. You won't have heard of us, we keep a pretty low profile.

The old lady shakes her head. No, I haven't, sorry.

Don't apologize, Mrs Sugden: like I said, we keep a low profile. There's a way you can help us though, if you will.

I will if I can, Miss . . .?

Craven. Veronica Craven. The thing is, for reasons that're too complicated to go into right now, I need to speak to somebody who was Dale Ward's friend. *Best* friend, preferably. She smiles. You'd know who he was, I dare say?

The lollipop lady nods. I know 'em all, Miss Craven. *All* my children. She pulls a face. I call them my children but I'm glad those Wards aren't mine, I'd die of shame.

Quite right. So what's his name, this best friend?

Colin Taylor. He's got a bike but he crosses with me. I'll tell him you want a word, shall I?

Thanks, Mrs Sugden: you'll be doing more than you know. She twinkles. More than that tanker would've done.

22

Uh . . . I'm Colin. Mrs Sugden says you want a word.

Yes, Colin, if you've got a few minutes. Shall we . . .? The journalist nods towards a nearby park. It'll be quieter there, might be a bench or something.

The boy nods. There is. He walks beside her, wheeling his bike.

This'll do nicely, says Minnie, choosing a seat half-hidden by rhododendron.

Colin leans his machine against one end and joins her. Youngsters pass by, walking or on bikes. There are curious glances. The boy looks uncomfortable. Can we get on with it? he mumbles.

Yes, of course. Minnie smiles. I expect you'll get ribbed tomorrow, eh, sitting in the park with a mysterious stranger?

Yeah.

Sorry, Colin. She introduces herself as Veronica from MOVE ON, which she says is an acronym: Murderers Owe Victims Everything, Offer Nothing. Says she's making inquiries about Dale Ward, understands he and Colin were friends. The boy nods.

That's why this is a hassle, see? I'm the school weirdo 'cause I used to go to Dale's house; they'll think I've brought you here to throttle you.

Surely not?

Well, they'll *pretend* to think that. He did one of 'em here, that Gavin.

Really?

Yeah, over there by the shelter.

How ghastly. So you were pretty close, you and Dale?

I suppose.

D'you keep in touch?

What, *now*? Course not, they went away. Had to.

Yes, I know. You've no idea *where*, I suppose?

No, how would I? They were hardly going to leave a whatsit: forwarding address.

That's right, Colin, but I thought Dale might have talked about a particular place: you know, before all this happened. Somewhere the family liked, perhaps.

Colin shakes his head. No, not that I remember. The dad went all over of course, fitting security stuff. Have you tried his firm?

Oh, yes. They had to sack him, don't know where he went.

What about prison?

The woman frowns. Prison?

Yeah, where Gavin is.

What about it, Colin?

They'll visit him, won't they, his mum and dad? If you went there and hung about, they'd be bound to show up sooner or later, then you follow 'em home. He

44

shrugs. Where they are, that's where you'll find Dale.

Good Lord! Minnie Cooper gawps at the boy. Now why the heck did that never occur to *me*? She chuckles, shaking her head. I'm losing it, must be. And as for you, young man, you're a genius. Here. She roots in her shoulder bag, pulls out a purse and peels off a ten pound note. Buy yourself . . . whatever. She laughs, gets to her feet. Far from throttling me, you've saved my life.

The boy looks from the banknote in his hand to the woman, hurrying away at the half-trot. Hey, just a minute, I can't . . .

Of *course* you can. Bye. She flings the words over her shoulder and disappears through the gateway.

An older boy passes, grinning. How's it work then, Taylor: ten quid not to do 'em in?

Colin groans, knowing it'll be all round school tomorrow.

23

Wednesdays I see my counsellor. Rolf, they call him. He's about thirty, shaves his head, wears jogging kit. His job's to keep me out of the nuthouse. We meet at half-seven in a bistro called the Crypt, which is under the parish church. He picked it because it's uncool, kids don't use it so I won't run into anybody from school. Plus it's darkish, which I like.

I can say anything to Rolf, it won't go any further. It took me a while to trust him but I do now. He brings the coffees over, sits down, grins. How's it hanging, Glen?

Straight down the middle, Rolf.

Great.

Same old worries though.

Really: you mean . . .?

I nod. *Am I normal*, yeah.

He pulls a face. Has something happened to . . . you know, set it off again, because you said last week you were handling it, remember?

I tell him about my attack on Hawthorne and what Waggy said after. He listens without butting in, he's good like that. I sigh. It's that bit, *Are you telling me you didn't know what you were doing?*, that's screwing me up, Rolf: it's like he knows who I am.

Rolf shakes his head. It's not that, Glen. He thought you were claiming to have blacked out or something, so you wouldn't be blamed.

You reckon?

Absolutely. Think about it: if he knew who you are he wouldn't just stop your privileges, he'd want you out of his school: safety of the other pupils and all that.

I suppose.

You bet he would. And like I told you the other week, your brother's condition has no hereditary component: it doesn't run in families as far as we know. You're a perfectly normal guy, Glen: a perfectly normal guy who lost his role model and had his whole world turned upside down, just when he was battling with the onset of adolescence. It's not surprising your confidence is shot, that you feel weird. I'd be climbing the wall if it were me.

Old Rolf. He's got a way of talking, a way of *sitting*, that relaxes you. He *gives off* calm, like listening to the sea. I can't imagine *anything* sending him up the wall. I want to just sit there quietly and absorb what's coming off him, but Waggy's words aren't my only hang-up.

There's a couple more things, Rolf: symptoms, I call 'em.

Symptoms? He arches his brow. Of what, mate?

Of not being . . . like everybody else.

Go on.

It's embarrassing, I don't know if I can . . .

He smiles. I'll have heard it before, Glen, whatever it is, because nobody's unique. Whatever you're feeling's been felt many times before, however bizarre it may seem. Tell me.

He's terrific, but all the same I'm glad it's dim in here. I couldn't tell this stuff in daylight, even to Rolf. I start with my dream: the one where I'm chasing Sally Prentice through a wood. He really listens, nods from time to time, doesn't laugh. If he laughed or even smiled, it'd be the end of it.

After the dream I tell him about Sally and Carla on the bench under the staffroom window, how they mocked me and what I fantasized doing to shut them up. I'm watching his eyes as I tell this last bit, looking for a flicker of concern that'll mean he's not sure about me. There's nothing, so then I move on to those other thoughts I have about Sally: the really embarrassing stuff he's bound to find seriously pervy. The phrase *products of a diseased imagination* springs to mind. The only way I can talk about it is to stare at the candle inside the little lamp in the middle of the table all the time I'm speaking.

I tell it all; if he knows the worst he can say what's wrong with me. I can't go on pretending to get on with life like everybody else, while uncertainty squats day and night like an ugly great toad at the back of my mind, spoiling everything. If I'm dangerous let them lock me up *now*, not after I've done Sally Prentice in and got my name all over the papers.

The silence when I finally stop stretches on and on. There's a green floating blob from staring at the candle. It stops me seeing anything else, but I can practically feel the handcuffs snapping shut.

24

In the end I have to break the silence, can't stand it. That bad, huh?

Uh? No, no. He shakes his head. Sorry, I was thinking. And it isn't bad, Glen, not in *any* way.

Relief flickers, but I hold it back, have to be sure. Those *thoughts*, Rolf, I murmur: about Sally and Carla and Miss Royd. Miss *Royd* for Pete's sake: she's ancient, what sort of a guy has dirty thoughts about someone *that* age? It's got to be sick, stuff like that.

No. He shakes his head. It isn't sick, mate, it's par for the course. Remember what I said a few minutes ago: *just when he was battling with the onset of adolescence*?

Yeah, I remember.

He shrugs, smiles. Well *that*'s the sort of guy who has thoughts like yours, Glen: an adolescent guy. *Every* adolescent guy.

Straight up, Rolf? You wouldn't shit me on this, 'cause it really *really* matters, y'know?

Of *course* it does. He reaches across, squeezes my shoulder. I wouldn't shit you, Glen, on this or anything else. You've got to stop thinking of yourself as a psychopath's apprentice, mate, because it just doesn't happen like that.

I sit back, sip coffee, chill out. This isn't the end of it, I know that. The toad of uncertainty will come crawling back some night when Rolf's not there. Rolf knows: says I can call him any time day or night, but I wouldn't. Not at night. If you can't take care of your own damn self for a few hours, you might as well give up.

We drink more coffee, chat a bit, then Rolf gets up to go. We never leave together. Sometimes I go first. He lifts a hand goodbye, at the foot of the old stone steps, and I nod. If anybody tries to tell you counselling's crap, ignore them.

As I drain my cup and push the chair back to get up, Will Tomlinson hails me. I'm not glad to see him and my response is muted to say the least, but better than he'd get from a dolmen I dare say. He strides over, grinning, shouts that he'd no idea I came in here and asks the whole place what I'm doing.

I was just going, I tell him as he plonks himself down on Rolf's chair. I've never been here before, thought I'd have a look.

And?

I shrug. Too quiet. Place for oldies. Shan't bother again.

Oh. He looks hurt. That's what I like about it, the quiet.

I nod. Come a lot then, do you?

Not a lot, no. Now and then.

Wednesdays?

He shakes his head. No, no, Saturday afternoons. I'm not usually in town evenings, only there was a lecture at the institute: 'Landscape and Legend' it was called, and Roger Fenby was giving it. It's just finished and I was thirsty, so here I am.

Ah. Good was it, the lecture?

Well what do *you* think? Roger Fenby.

Don't know him.

I'll lend you one of his books, I've got them all.

No, it's OK. I grin. Enough with *Wuthering Heights*, eh?

Oh, Fenby's books aren't like *that*, Glen. They're slim volumes, local history. He puts jokes in them.

Local history jokes?

Yes.

They'll be hilarious then.

They *are*. I'll bring one to school tomorrow.

Thanks.

Have you ever noticed how enthusiastic people don't recognize sarcasm if it's directed at their subject?

25

I always feel better for talking to Rolf, but even he can't make the whole thing go away. Leaving the Crypt, I pass a girl crossing the churchyard and check myself for unnatural urges. There are none, unless you count the urge to check yourself for unnatural urges, but biking home in the dark I think about her, imagining what might have happened if it'd been Gav instead of me and that's what I mean: it never goes away.

The randomness is part of the horror. My brother didn't select his victims in advance: it all depended on who was nearby when it came over him, whatever *it* is. Somebody decides she'll take a shortcut through a churchyard or pee in some bushes: some seemingly tiny choice, and sheer chance makes it the last decision of her life.

The list of Gav's victims is one of the things I can't stop thinking about. I memorized it without meaning to, in chronological order, during the trial. Here it is:

- Sarah Lang, twenty
- Virginia Mason, seventeen
- Sally Halifax, twenty
- Crystal Ball, thirty-eight
- Caroline Summers, eighteen

I didn't know any of these women. The papers printed snapshots, but snaps of murder victims always seem to be of poor quality somehow, so I don't know what they were really like. What I know is, each one of them was precious to somebody, and maybe that's the only difference between Gav and me: he doesn't see it.

I think about these women, who aren't women any more because of my brother. Some of my thoughts are pretty much what you'd expect: what were they like when they were my sister's age; what did they hope to be; what kids'll never be born because they're dead? It gets weird after that, because then there's the kids those unborn kids would've had, then *their* kids, and I end up wondering just how many lives Gav *prevented*, on top of the five he snuffed out. Must be hundreds. He might have robbed the world of a Mozart or a John Logie Baird. On the other hand he might've prevented a Hitler or a Doctor Shipman, in which case five deaths might be a small price . . .

Does your head in, stuff like that. And I catch myself thinking disrespectful crap as well, such as I hope Mr and Mrs Ball managed to hang on to the sense of humour that made them call their kid Crystal, 'cause they need it now.

All this plays back for the thousandth time inside my head as I cycle home. I love my big brother, I *do*, but, you know, I sometimes wish he'd never been born.

26

Oh, hi, Glen, I've brought the Fenby. He flaps the thing in my face so I miss the wheel-slot twice. I'd tell the irritating sod to shove off, but I walked out on him a bit abruptly last night and I've got a conscience.

I finish with the bike, straighten up and take the book. Thanks, Will.

'S all right. He beams. You're in for a treat, and I don't need it back anytime soon. His smile fades. You left in a bit of a hurry last night, I hope you weren't mad at me.

No, no, I lie, shaking my head. I didn't like the place and I was knackered, that's all. Did you stay long?

'Bout ten minutes. He frowns. Was somebody with you before I showed up, Glen?

My heart kicks me in the ribs. No, why?

He shrugs. Guy comes over just after you went, he'd left his document case. It was against the wall by my foot. He must've sat there before me.

I nod. Must've.

You didn't *see* him: slaphead, thirtyish, jogging kit?

Not to notice, no. *Change the subject for Pete's sake.* I tap the book. Funny title, *Watch the Wall My Darling*. Why's it called that?

He smiles. 'Cause it's about smuggling.

So?

Don't tell me you've never heard Kipling's poem, 'The Smuggler's Song'?

No, but I've eaten his cakes a few times.

Oh, very funny. He grows serious. It was the smuggling capital of the West Country in the old days, y'know, Market Flaxton. Booze, mostly. There were shoot-outs between smugglers and customs officers. It's all in there.

Super.

I *said* you were in for a treat.

I plough through the thing in my room the same evening. Thirty pages, feels like a hundred. Roger Fenby must be the only man on earth who can take an exciting subject like smuggling and write about it so boringly it's like reading the history of underpants from 200 BC to the present day. He *does* use jokes though. Here's a sample: a magistrate is being driven to court in his coach and pair. He's due to try a notorious smuggler and he's running late. He orders the coachman to hurry. On a sharp bend, the coach casts a wheel and overturns. *A grave miscarriage of justice*, quips Fenby. I laugh so much I stop breathing, have to be rushed to hospital and resuscitated.

Not.

27

Let me get this straight, Minnie. You've drawn a blank, so you think you deserve a late-season break on the Isle of Wight, all expenses paid. Is that it?

Well, I wouldn't put it *quite* like that, DP. It won't be . . .

I would, and it's open-ended too. Nice little village, room at the local pub, sit and wait till the Wards decide to visit their ogre son. It could be a month. Two months. Nice work if you can get it, young woman.

I've tried everything else, DP. Ex-neighbours, ex-best friends, ex-employers: nothing. It's like they were snatched by aliens. I phoned the Home Office about visiting orders, got nowhere. Oh, they'll tell you what a visiting order *is* and how the system works, but the minute they suss you're interested in a particular inmate, the shutters come down.

Well, of course they do, you silly girl, you could be *anybody*: part of a plot to spring that particular inmate, get him out of the country. It's happened. You've got to use a bit of ingenuity, Minnie, bit of imagination.

I *am*, DP. I don't plan to sit and wait. There'll be off-duty prison officers, civilian employees. I'll get into conversation, loosen somebody up, dig a bit. I don't think it'll take a month, don't *want* it to: I have my own life.

So *do* it, Minnie, but don't take the penthouse suite.

No oysters and champagne on room service, d'you hear?

Oysters? Ugh!

And if you're caught bribing a prison officer, the *Post*'s never heard of you.

28

Friday morning a buff envelope drops on the mat. There aren't many good things about our situation, but one is that the senders of junk mail have lost track of us for now and the envelope has the mat to itself. Mum brings it to the breakfast table. We know what's inside before she opens it. It's a visiting order, which you need before you can go and see somebody in prison.

The twenty-fourth, says Mum when she's looked at it.

Next Tuesday, says Dad. Short notice, that.

Mum nods, but she'll go. If it was today she'd find a way of getting there, that's how mothers are. I'll need Monday off, she says. Kathleen won't mind. Kathleen's boss of the tourist-information centre, she's all right.

What'll you tell her? asks Dad.

Mum pulls a face. Our Maureen again, I suppose. Maureen's my invisible auntie, Mum's imaginary sister. She's an invalid, lives up north and comes in handy.

Ah, well mind you don't come it too brown, growls Dad. He means don't overdo it, use the same excuse too often. He loves Gav, but thinks Mum lives too much for these visits. The Isle of Wight's a long way off: she comes home shattered, not to mention upset.

It's from Gavin, isn't it? goes Kirsty. That letter.

Yes, love, smiles Mum, and he says I'm to give his little sister a great big hug from him. She gets up, comes round the table and hugs Kirsty from behind so the kid won't see the tears in her eyes.

When's he coming home? she asks when Mum's through hugging her.

Oh, I don't know, love: he's busy you see, driving his truck all over the world. He's thinking about us though, every minute: 'specially *you*.

She thinks Gav's doing some sort of long-haul delivery, our Kirsty. Well, you can't tell a kid that age, can you? I envy her sometimes, the picture she must have in her mind of her big brother, rolling along some endless highway with the window down and the music up. Wish that were what *I* saw.

People cheered, you know. In court, when the judge sent him to prison. They were glad he got prison, not a secure hospital. And these weren't victims' families, I'd understand *them* being glad, cheering even, but no: these were just people in the public gallery, people he hadn't done anything to at all. It obviously didn't occur to any of them that it could just as easily be *their* son in the dock, *their* brother. None of them stopped to think how *we* were feeling: how they'd feel if it was them.

There's more bad people out of jail than in.

29

First period Friday, Shikey rubs his hands at us. Now, he says briskly, who *hasn't* managed to get hold of a copy of *Wuthering Heights*? Four hands go up, three belonging to the Mafia. Shikey's got some beat-up paperbacks, dishes them out to the dark quartet. Right. He grins like a shark. Who's actually *read* it?

Will shoots his hand up. Everybody groans. Get a life, Tomlinson, growls Hawthorne, but I'm not surprised. Compared to Fenby on smuggling, old Emily's Stephen King and Terry Pratchett rolled into one.

Good man, says Shikey. Did you notice anything strange about the author's narrative technique?

Will's stumped, which serves him right. Uh . . . how d'you mean, sir, technique? Sniggers in various quarters.

Shikey tries to make it simpler. How she chooses to *tell* the story, Tomlinson.

Uh . . . no, sir, not particularly.

Do we get it directly from *her*, tries Shikey, being dead patient. Is Emily Brontë our *narrator*?

Dunno, sir: do you mean did she *write* it?

No, no, no, laddie, of course she *wrote* it. I'm talking about technique here: surely you understand the word technique?

The look on Will's face, he's wishing he'd kept his hand

down. The kids're giggling like mad. Feeling sorry for the sad plonker I stick my hand up.

Yes, Parish?

Sir, it's told at two removes: Nellie Dean's telling Lockwood the story, so the author's keeping well out of it.

Shikey's surprised. He tries not to show it, but he is. He probably expected a load of bullshit from the new boy, not the right answer. It nearly chokes him, but he nods and says, That's correct, Parish: it's told at two removes, a complex and unusual technique.

I do my modest smile and Hawthorne stage-whispers, You're dead at break, Parish, no danger. Shikey hears but doesn't intervene. Instead he looks at me and says, Work that out for yourself did you, Parish?

I wish I could claim to have worked it out, but I can't. I shake my head. No, sir, we did *Wuthering Heights* at my other school.

Did you? He looks surprised again. I'd have thought it was a bit advanced for thirteen-year-olds.

I nod. We didn't read it, sir, we sort of talked about it, along with the other Brontë novels. We were doing a topic about them.

Oh? Why's that, Parish?

He's luring me into dangerous waters, but I don't notice, too busy showing off. I'm like, Oh, well, the Brontës are very big round our way, sir. There's even a Brontë tandoori, if you can believe it.

Hmm. He looks at me. So you're actually *from* Haworth?

Now I notice, now that it's too late. I shake my head. No, sir, we lived miles away. Miles and miles but I've *been*. You know, visited. With school, and with my mum and dad. It's a favourite place of theirs.

Yes, I see. Shikey nods. He doesn't push and the lesson continues, but I'm wishing I'd kept my big mouth shut.

Nobody likes a smartass.

30

Hey, Glen, thanks for the rescue act.

It's breaktime, I'm in the doorway of the science block keeping my eyes skinned for the Mafia when Will finds me.

I smile. 'S OK, Will, you're welcome.

He pulls a rueful face. Last time *I* stick my hand up for old Shikey, I can tell you: what a wonka.

Yeah. Oh, I brought your book back. I hand him the Fenby borathon.

He grins. Good, isn't it?

'S right, Will: good isn't it.

What d'you *mean*?

Well. I shake my head. The guy takes an interesting topic like smuggling and makes it as dry as double maths. I mean, there must've been fights, betrayals, ambushes. People must've drowned or been shot. Snitches beaten up, guys tortured, stuff like that, but there's hardly any of it in the book. It's all statistics: how many kegs of brandy, pounds of tobacco, casks of wine. How much dosh was lost to the ex-flipping-chequer. Who *cares* for Pete's sake? And as for the jokes, they're about as funny as a kick in the crutch with a foundryman's clog.

He's hurt, I can tell by his face, but if I said I enjoyed the bloody thing he'd bring more, wouldn't he, and I'd have to go on lying, and I lie enough already. I shrug. Different people like different things, Will, right? It's not my cup of tea, doesn't mean it's no good.

He doesn't say anything. I think he'd have walked away if Hawthorne and his buddies hadn't picked that moment to show up. Look, Den, goes Baird, it's the Siamese twins.

Hawthorne leers at me. *Sir*, he bleats in a sheep's voice, *it's told at two removes*. His lip curls. *I'll show you two removes, you slimy creep: grab 'em!*

He wants us in the bins, of course, only there's two of us this time and we go back-to-back to make it as hard for them as we can. I *know* I said I wouldn't lose it again, but I'm not starting this am I? Being in the doorway means the three of them can't rush us at the same time: it's one-on-one. Baird lashes out at me with his Nike and I manage to grab his foot. With the toe in one hand and the heel in the other I twist with all my strength. He follows to keep it from breaking and falls on his face. Hawthorne darts in to take his sidekick's place, grabbing two fistfuls of my hair. I get him by the throat and we force each other's heads back. He's trying to knee me in the groin, but Baird's under his feet, he can't get the right stance. I'm pressing my thumbs into his Adam's apple and trying to get my knee in first, but Baird's in my way too. Will keeps pressing into my back as he tussles with Wilson.

I'm holding my own with Hawthorne: might even be winning, because while I can ignore the pain in my scalp, he can't fight without oxygen and my thumbs've all but cut off his supply. He's making gagging noises; I can feel him weakening. One more big effort and he'll back off or black out, no other option. It's then I think of Gav with his hands round a throat, squeezing the life out of somebody's sister. *He* must've felt the surge of fierce joy I'm feeling as his victim's struggles began to fail. *He* didn't want to stop, wouldn't stop till . . .

Horrified, I let go. Baird crawls clear, Hawthorne grunts as his knee slams into my groin. Blinding pain convulses me, nothing else exists. I don't even know I'm down. Somebody shouts, guys're squealing, running. I'm curled, one ear on rough cement, fighting to breathe. My middle's nothing but pain, which breathing aggravates. The tussle seems to have stopped and there's a wet noise, snuffling or crying or both. Something screens out the light, it goes colder, everything recedes . . .

31

Parish, can you hear me?

I can hear him. Shann, boys' PE.

Squeeze my hand if you can hear me.

He's holding my flipping hand. I squeeze.

Good lad, you'll be fine.

I don't feel fine. I've thrown up on the step, the right side of my face is in it, but at least the pain in my middle is shrinking, now it's just my groin.

Parish?

Uuuh. I open my left eye, the other won't. Sir?

You've had a nasty kick but nothing seems to be broken. D'you think you can sit up if I help you?

I can sit up, sir, don't need help. I don't want Shann's help, he gets the kids laughing when somebody can't vault the buck. I heave, prop myself on one elbow, moan as nausea sweeps through me. Shann swabs my eye with a tissue. It opens, fragments of puke on the lashes look like asteroids. My groin's on fire.

Come on, lad, let's get you up. He shoves his hands into my armpits and lifts me on to my feet. I don't know why he's in such a rush, I'm not ready. There's another bout of nausea, it's as much as I can do not to puke down the front of his tracksuit. As it is, my head lolls on his shoulder like he's dancing with a drunk. I feel a total prat, but there's nothing I can do about it. And, of course, there's a big audience. Shann pulls my arm across his shoulders and starts walking me very slowly towards the main building. My knackers are the size of grapefruit, and throb like crazy. The crowd parts in front of us like the Red Sea.

We're headed for the first-aid room. Shann and the secretary help me lie down. The secretary's Mrs Waverley. She gives me a smile, drops a red blanket over me and goes off to tell the head, and to find her pad of accident forms.

Shann pulls up a chair, sits down and looks at me. Who's Caroline, Parish?

Caroline? My heart kicks. I try to look puzzled, keep my voice level. I don't know a Caroline, sir.

He pulls a face. Funny, you were jabbering away thirteen to the dozen when I reached you, apologizing to somebody called Caroline. At least it *sounded* like Caroline. Sorry, Caroline, you were saying. Sorry, Caroline, over and over.

It's Caroline Summers, of course, my brother's last victim. The thought of her throat caving in under his thumbs made me let go of Hawthorne's. I remember that, but I'd no idea I'd spoken her name: aren't aware of having spoken at all. I shake my head.

Must've been a sort of dream, sir.

Shann nods. Delirious, perhaps. He grins. I thought maybe you were apologizing to your girlfriend for the state of your equipment.

He's a tosser is Shann, but in the circumstances I'm happy enough to dismiss the incident this way. I even manage a chuckle, which hurts my equipment a bit.

32

The nights are drawing in. It always used to depress me, the way evenings shrink after mid-August. You're no sooner home from school than it's starting to get dark, and by the time it's light again you're back in the classroom.

Bit different this year though. For us I mean. Sunlight's the enemy when you're trying to hide: you're a black beetle crossing a floodlit floor, a louse on a hospital sheet. You want a dark corner.

So, as the days grow shorter my family starts to unwind a bit. We've been three months in Market Flaxton; people're getting so used to seeing us they don't see us any more, and there's less and less daylight to see us by. We're melting into the foreground.

On Saturday, Mum, Kayleigh and I drive out to the supermarket where Dad works: Caffyn's. We're not there specially to see Dad: the job's a come-down from his old one and he feels daft in the uniform, but all the employees' families shop there and we don't want to stick out as different.

I wheel our trolley through the automatic doors and there he is in his peaked cap, watching for grazers on the fruit and veg aisle. Kayleigh slips Mum's hand, runs to him. She's dry at night now, a happy little girl again. Dad opens his arms and scoops her up.

Mum's off to see Gav Tuesday. She'll take fruit, chocolate, a juice drink. I nod to Dad on my way to the nibbles, where I pick up six packs of salted cashews for my brother. He's always been mad on salted cashews. I'd go with Mum, give them to him myself, but he doesn't want me visiting, says he couldn't stand it. To be perfectly honest I don't know if I could either.

I've collected the nuts and found Mum by the bananas

when Shann appears. He's by himself, carrying a basket. I develop a sudden interest in redcurrants, hoping he won't spot me, but he already has.

He approaches. Morning, Parish. He's one of those people who talks as though the whole world wants to know his business. This lady your mum?

Y . . . Yessir. Mum, this is Mr Shann from school, takes us for PE.

Oh, goes Mum. Pleased to meet you, Mr Shann. She isn't. It's like parking your trolley under a foghorn, everybody's looking.

Pleasure's mine, Mrs Parish. Just wondered how your lad's doing after yesterday's little incident.

Incident? She doesn't know what he's talking about because I haven't mentioned my run-in with Hawthorne. Never mind: the whole supermarket'll know in a minute.

Oh, hasn't he told you, the rascal? One of our more physical pupils kneed him in a very tender spot, I had to render first aid.

Mum looks at me. You never mentioned . . .

I shake my head. I didn't want you worrying, that's all. I turn to Shann. I'm fine, sir, thanks. *Go away*, I'm thinking. *Stop drawing attention*.

Good, he booms. No further visitation from the mysterious Caroline then, eh?

Mum looks startled. Caroline? Who's . . .?

It's OK, Mum, I hallucinated, just for a second. A girl. It must've been the pain.

Shann nods. There's no pain like it, Mrs Parish, you can take it from me. Well . . . he looks at me. Glad to see you

66

fully operational again, Parish. He nods to Mum. Nice to have met you, Mrs Parish: I expect we'll be seeing you at one of our parents' events. Goodbye.

Goodbye, Mr Shann, goes Mum. Thanks for . . . you know, the first aid.

Part of the job, he grins. See you Monday, Parish.

He strides off swinging his basket. I don't suppose everybody really *has* stopped to watch and listen: it's just that the bustle seems to start up again as he disappears. I steer the trolley into it, seeking that dark corner I mentioned.

Mum, hurrying at my side, plucks at my sleeve. Caroline, she murmurs, was one of the girls our Gav . . .

Let's not go there, Mum. I speak more sharply than I mean to.

33

She's off at the crack of dawn, Monday, in the used Polo Dad bought when we moved here. She wants to be on the island by teatime; she's booked a room at a pub in Newport, which is handy for the prison.

Dad's arranged a lift with a guy he works with, which leaves me to get Kayleigh to school. It's a short walk. I push the bike with one hand, hold hers in the other. Where's Mum gone? she asks as we turn out of the Avenue. I trot out the story we've concocted.

Auntie Maureen's poorly again, Mum's gone to see if she can help.

Have I seen Auntie Maureen?

Yes, but you probably don't remember: it was when you were really small.

Where does she live?

Oh, way up north: much further than our old place. That's why Mum'll be away overnight.

What's wrong with her?

Auntie Maureen? I dunno, love: something women get I expect.

Will she die?

No, no, it's not that bad: she can't always manage shopping and ironing and stuff, that's all, so Mum does it for her.

Oh.

I hate lying to the kid. *Hate* it, but there's no other way. You can't tell a seven-year-old her mum visits her big brother in jail and expect her to keep it a secret. Takes *me* all my time.

We approach Highfield Primary just as the lollipop lady lets a mob of kids cross. A little lass calls out to Kayleigh, waits by the gate.

Who's this? I ask as we draw near.

Stephanie, my best friend. She's got a spaniel puppy at home called Frankie. Hi, Steph!

Hi, Kayleigh. The child gives me a puzzled glance and Kayleigh responds. I've come with Glen this morning, my brother.

Oh, hi. I rate a shy smile.

Hi, Stephanie, how's Frankie?

Uh . . . he's OK thanks. You can see her thinking, *How the heck does he know Frankie?*

Good. I nod and smile. Off you go then, the pair of you: I want to see you safe inside that playground before I leave. They give me a look, then run off hand in hand, giggling.

It amazes me how a little kid can adjust like my sister has. She *isn't* Kayleigh, she's Kirsty, yet she responds to Kayleigh easily and naturally, as though it's always been her name. And she introduces me as Glen so you can't see the join. Incredible.

I mount up and weave through the morning traffic, happy that my sister's found a friend, wondering if Gav has. In the absence of any other hope, I hope he's managing to adjust too, so that perhaps his life's not quite as terrible as I imagine it being. I can't see him lasting long if it is.

And with that cheerful thought I toil up Tanner Hill to school.

34

Sally, goes Shikey to the gorgeous Miss Prentice, do you remember the question you asked the day I told the class we were going to be looking at this novel? He taps his copy of *Wuthering Heights*.

Sally wrinkles her brow: nobody's at their brightest first thing Monday. Uh . . . no, sir.

It was about the title, clues Shikey.

The penny drops. Oh . . . oh yeah. I asked what it meant, sir.

What *what* meant, Sally?

Sir, wuthering.

And what was my answer?

Something about weather, sir: wet and windy, wasn't it?

It was indeed, he smiles, which brings me neatly to our task for today, which is to examine Emily Brontë's use of atmospheric phenomena in the novel. Tell me, Hawthorne: what, in the course of your no doubt close reading of the text, did you notice about the author's use of atmospheric phenomena?

Uh . . . ah . . . *eh*?

Are you speaking some obscure dialect version of English, Hawthorne?

Ah . . . no, I'm thinking, sir.

Splendid: take your time.

I . . . don't know, sir.

You don't know. Shikey gives him an accusing look. Yours hasn't been a *close* reading at all, has it, lad?

No, sir.

In fact, it hasn't even been a quick reading, am I right?

Yes, sir.

Have you *skip*-read the book, you semicolon?

Yes, sir.

No you haven't. You haven't even *opened* it, have

you? It's been lying on whatever flat surface it landed on when you skimmed it across the room the day you took it home, right?

Yes, sir.

Yes, sir, goes Shikey. He's got us all laughing; he's enjoying himself. First thing tomorrow morning, lad, he says to Hawthorne, I want you to come and tell me what Heathcliff overhears Cathy saying, which causes him to leave Wuthering Heights. His eyes rake the class. And don't *anybody* tell him, understand?

Nods round the room, mumbles of, Yes, sir. Hawthorne opens his copy and scans the publisher's blurb in the desperate hope of finding the answer there. *I* know it, but my motto from now on is a low profile at all times. No more showing off. If Shikey asks me anything, *anything* about the book or the Brontës, I'll play dumb.

Heathcliff was able to come back in the end: we'd have to go away forever.

35

At lunchtime I trek with my mobile to the remotest corner of the playing field and call Rolf. I get his answering machine, wait for the beep. Oh, Rolf, it's Glen. Bit of a prob. This lad at school, Will Tomlinson: the one I mentioned to you because he talks to me? He showed up at the Crypt last week, just after you left. You saw him when you went back for your document case, he was at our table. The thing is, he asked me if I'd been with some-one before he arrived. I said no, of course, but he's the sort of guy who might swing by again, same night only earlier, to try and catch me out. I was wondering if it might be best for us to meet somewhere else. You've got my number, I'll be home around four, you can call anytime after that. Cheers.

Talk of the devil: I've hardly broken the connection and here he comes, grinning like a loony. Phoning some-body, Glen?

No, I pick my teeth with this.

Oh ha-flipping-ha, just 'cause you've got a small phone. Who was it?

Tony Blair, I'm his education adviser.

All right *don't* tell me, see if I care.

I look at him. There's a mouse under his left eye where Wilson smacked him. I should lighten up a bit, he got clobbered for being with me. I smile, shake my head. Some things *are* private you know, Will.

He shrugs. Whatever, I was just making conversation.

I nod. Listen, tomorrow's young teens night at Hangovers, right?

It is.

D'you fancy giving it a go?

Me? He shakes his head. I don't do clubbing, Glen, I thought you knew that.

Well, yeah, but like, you could make an exception for once: you never know, you might get to like it.

I doubt it, thudding bass and strobes. Vodka.

No *vodka*, dummy, not on young teens. Sally and Carla might be there.

And what's the use of that? They laugh at you, you said so.

Yeah, but that's 'cause they've never seen me in pulling mode. They'll be all over me when I boogie up to 'em in my coolest kit.

He pulls a face. That's another thing, I don't have cool stuff.

I grin. Show up in your go-to-lecture get-up, it might catch on.

Oh sure: corduroy sports coat, row of pens in the top pocket. Next big thing.

Well. I shrug. *I'm* going.

Good luck. Anyway there's a documentary on the box: *Riddle of the Desert Mummies*. Can't miss that.

No. I shake my head. Treat of a lifetime, I should think. Hawthorne and his mates'll be glued to it.

D'you *think* so?

Course not, you lymphocyte: mummies *think* too fast for Hawthorne.

Will smiles. The buzzer goes. We stroll back across the field.

36

I'm getting Kayleigh's tea when my moby chirps. Yeah?

Hi, Glen: Rolf.

Oh, hi, you got my message.

Yes. Look, how likely is it that this Will character'll show up at The Crypt?

Well I dunno, I just thought he might.

He's a bit of a wimp, isn't he? Is he in town much at night?

No, no, he's more your computer and telly man. Some loony called Fenby was giving a lecture last week, he was up for that.

Right. Reason I ask, I've had situations like this before. The thing is, you can run into someone you know *wherever* you go, and if you switch venues every time you're gonna run out of places in the end. I'd be inclined to stick with the Crypt, mate. If your pal *does* shows up we tell him we're Yorkshiremen in exile, talking about God's own county. He chuckles. Make a *lamp post* walk away, that would.

Yeah, but like, can you do the accent?

Course ah can, thi claatheead.

Who was that? asks Kayleigh. She's had to wait for her pizza. I slip my hands into the oven glove. Guy I talk to sometimes, love: from Yorkshire like us.

Oh.

I dish up and we eat. There's just the two of us: Dad won't be back till six. It's always pizza when Mum's away, or something else you just heat up. There's a treacle tart to follow so Kayleigh's happy: she'd not get two pastry dishes if Mum were here.

Drivers rolling off the Isle of Wight ferry are confronted with a sign that reads: ISLAND ROADS ARE DIFFERENT. Passing this gentle reminder, Anna Parish smiles tiredly, imagining how happy she'd be if this were home or the start of a holiday, as it is for the occupants of most of the cars ahead of her and behind. Here, nobody will hoot or flash his lights as she cruises at thirty along bendy, narrow roads between high hedges. There'll be no tailgater like the idiot who harassed her this morning on the mainland. You *feel* the difference the minute you leave the terminal, but for Anna the feeling is marred by the purpose of her visit and the need for secrecy. *My son lives here*, she's imagined herself telling some curious fellow passenger on the ferry. True, yet monstrously untrue.

She hangs a left for Newport where she'll shower, eat and rest. Or not rest. Anna loves all three of her children, unconditionally and forever, and that's her tragedy.

37

Tuesday. 09.35 by my deceptively complicated digital watch. Four forty-nine it cost, in Poundstretcher. Spinal's droning on about phagocytes and lymphocytes and flipping *webcytes* for all I know, I'm not listening. Gav's watch is a Rolex, bottom of the range but a real one, and they won't let him have it. It's in a cardboard box along with his civvy clothes: Nikes and whatever else he had on him the day he was remanded. His property, they call it, but it's stashed away where he can't touch it till he gets out. Mum visits at eleven this morning, and one of the things she's going to do is ask if we can do a swap: Gav's Rolex for the piece of crap on my wrist. Apparently they let you have your watch if it's a cheap one, because you won't be able to sell it for tobacco or something. Anyway, Gav misses having a watch so she's going to ask.

Parish!

Y . . . Yes, Miss?

Did you even *hear* my question? I said, What special capability do leucocytes possess which renders them indispensable to us?

Leucocytes, Miss? They . . . *I don't flipping know, why pick on me?* They carry oxygen, Miss, to the brain.

Spinal compresses her lips. Leucocytes do *not* carry oxygen, Parish, to the brain or anywhere else. *Erythrocytes* do that, though probably not in your case, where the brain is a vestigial organ having no practical function.

It's laugh at Parish time again. I gaze out of the window wearing my *don't give a stuff* expression till they get over it. If they're so clever, how come they don't know I'm *not* Parish? How's this thick northern clod fooling them, all day every day?

All right, goes Spinal, that's enough. She's shown what

a comedian she is, time to get back to business. She glowers at me. For your especial benefit, Parish, I will repeat: leucocytes have the ability to ingest or destroy dead or foreign matter in the bloodstream. They are an essential part of the *immune* system. *What* are they an essential part of, Parish?

The immune system, Miss. I say it in my *all water off a duck's back* drone, keeping my face expressionless.

Marvellous! She beams at the class. You see: life *is* to be found, even in the most barren environments.

Parkhurst's a barren environment and my brother's got life in it, which is why I find it hard to get excited about leucocytes right now. This thought comes to me and I ache to say it but I can't.

I can't.

38

Minnie Cooper doesn't drive a Mini Cooper. Her car's a white Polo, and it turns into the visitors' car park behind a Mondeo and ahead of a Yaris. There are four people in the Mondeo, two in the Yaris. As she slots the Polo into a space, Minnie is pleased to see that several knots of people are loitering near vehicles, presumably waiting for the reception building to open.

It isn't really a building, it's one of those portable things like the loos they have at pop festivals, and it stands on an expanse of tarmac outside the prison gates. Ramps at either end lead up to doors which are closed. The word IN is stencilled on the rail of the near ramp, OUT on the rail of the other. Two prison officers lean either side of the IN sign, smoking. Neither glances towards the car park, which is filling up.

To visit somebody in prison you need a visiting order. Minnie Cooper hasn't got one because she doesn't know anybody in prison. She knows one or two people who *ought* to be in prison, but that's beside the point. She knows she won't get through the gates, but that's all right, she doesn't need to. All she needs is for one of Gavin Ward's parents to show up. Or both. She knows what they look like, she had plenty of time to study them in court. She hopes it'll be today, because it's the sixth time in seven days she's come here. This is a top-security prison: sooner or later somebody's bound to notice and challenge her.

Five minutes before reception is due to open, visitors drift towards the foot of the ramp and a queue forms. Minnie watches from the driving seat but sees no face she knows. She's practically resigned herself to the necessity of risking a seventh vigil when an old red Polo scrunches past and noses into a nearby space. The driver's door opens and out gets Anna Ward, wearing the coat she wore to the trial. She looks older.

39

Hi, Dad, how'd it go today? Ten past six, he's just walked in.

Same as usual, son. Mum not back?

She phoned, caught in the teatime rush. Should be in anytime now.

Where's Kayleigh?

Guess.

Watching telly?

Correct. There's quiche and baked spuds in the oven, green beans on top. We've had ours.

Sounds terrific, Glen: you'll be a celebrity chef before we know it, but I think I'll wait for Mum if that's all right. He hangs his jacket and cap on the newel post and goes upstairs. Seconds later Mum walks in.

Hi, Mum, how is he?

Oh. She shakes her head. He's how you'd expect him to be in that . . . place. She drops the car keys on the table, bursts into tears.

Aw, *Mum* . . I put my arms round her. Don't. Don't be upset. *What a pathetic thing to say.* Come on; sit down and I'll make you a nice cup of tea, you must be shattered.

She shakes her head. I don't want tea, Glen, I want my . . . my . . .

Anna. Dad crosses to her, kneels to take her in his arms. It was bad, sweetheart: I know. *I* should've gone, not you.

No! She shakes her head. He's *my* baby, *I* fed him and washed him and loved him, I have to be near him when . . . when they'll let me. She wails so loudly, Dad has to cover her mouth. The neighbours . . .

It's rotten, hearing your mum howl and not being able to do anything. *Say* anything, even. What can you say? *Shush, it's all right: your kid's going to spend the rest of his life in a six-by-ten cell, shitting in a bucket and getting pushed around by a bunch of little Hitlers, but hey – it's still a beautiful world.*

She stops after a while: gets control. She eats a bit of quiche, a bean or two. Kayleigh thinks something bad's happened to Auntie Maureen so I lie to her again: Mum's overtired from the journey, that's all, Auntie Maureen's fine. When the kid's gone to bed Mum tells us about Gav: how unhappy he looks, how pale. He puts on a cheerful front, she says: upbeat messages to Dad, Kayleigh and me about how he'll be back with us before we know it, bowling. But he won't live long, buried alive. You've only to look at him.

I'm supposed to be checking out Hangovers tonight, but with Mum the way she is I haven't the heart to mention it. We sit gawping at the telly, and it's not till bedtime she mentions the girl in the white Polo.

40

Where the heck's she got to? Visiting time's over, people're dispersing across the car park and there's no Anna Ward. She watches as vehicles start up, reverse in clouds of exhaust and roll in procession towards the exit. A couple of minutes and the spaces around her are empty, the white Polo conspicuous as a single tooth in an otherwise empty mouth.

Drat! There's just the two cars now, her own and Anna Ward's. It's a major blow to Minnie's plan, which is to follow her victim unnoticed to the ferry terminal and cross to the mainland on the same boat. Now, when the bloody woman *does* show up, she's bound to notice the only other vehicle on the park, especially since it's a Polo like her own. The only thing she can do is move, repark in a far corner where she'll be a bit less obvious, but what if she's under surveillance? Prison car park: there's bound to be cameras somewhere. It'll seem a bit strange won't it, visitor reparking instead of heading home?

In fact the decision is taken from her hands. As she dithers, a door in the prison gate opens and Anna Ward emerges. Minnie pulls a face. *Best stay put now.* She pretends to root in the door pocket as the other woman passes behind.

At this point Anna's consciousness barely registers

the presence of the other car, she's too blazingly angry. Having approached a prison officer about swapping Gavin's Rolex for the cheap watch she'd brought with her, she'd been told to wait while he found somebody more senior. She'd stood for fifteen minutes in a bare little room, only to be told when the senior officer eventually appeared that it was out of the question. When she'd tried to argue, he'd turned on her as though *she* were an inmate, shouting that he'd more than enough to do without making special arrangements so some pervert could ponce about smothered in jewellery, and who the blankety-blank did she think she was: Bianca bleat'n Jagger?

It's only when she's reversed out of her space and engaged first gear that she notices the other car in her rear-view mirror. It's just backed out, and its driver seems to be waiting for her to proceed. This is ordinary courtesy and she'd think nothing of it except that instead of following close behind as would normally happen, the young woman hangs back, fiddling with her sun visor though the sky's overcast. It's only when Anna reaches the exit and signals right that the white Polo rolls forward.

Alarm bells ring in Anna's head. *Why didn't the woman drive off like everybody else: she must've left the prison at the same time. And why's she hanging back now, does she intend to follow me? Why? Who is she?*

She drives at twenty, looking in the mirror. The Polo noses out, turns right and follows. Ahead, a fingerpost points out a narrow road on the left. Anna doesn't signal but takes the turn abruptly. The name on the post means nothing to her, this road's en route to nowhere. She keeps her eyes fixed on the mirror, and when the other car turns in she knows the worst.

41

It's little more than a track, serpentine between overgrown hedges: thirty's about as fast as you can go. Anna hunches over the wheel, eyes switching constantly between the road ahead and her rear-view mirror. The young woman's keeping a gap of about 100 metres, so that half the time the drivers can't see each other for bends. There are no turnings, except into field gates. Anna thinks briefly of driving into one of these to see what her pursuer will do, but rejects the idea: it's scary being followed, but bringing the episode to a head might be worse.

The village comes suddenly. A bend like all the others and without warning she's heading straight for the ancient chestnut in the middle of the green. She brakes, swerves left to follow the road and finds it goes no further. It's a loop, throwing a noose round the green before going back the way it came. She follows it round, passing her startled pursuer.

To her surprise there's no glimpse of the white Polo as she twists and turns to the main road. *Maybe she wasn't following me at all: maybe she lives in that village. I am paranoid, it could all have been my imagination.*

*

She hangs a left and heads for the ferries, checking her mirror every few seconds. No white Polo.

But ten minutes later relief turns to alarm when she emerges from the ticket office to find the vehicle six places behind her own in the queue to board. There can be no doubt now that the young woman is following her. Anna's immediate impulse is to confront her, demand to know who she is and what the hell she thinks she's playing at. Her window's down, she's lounging behind the wheel wearing shades and pretending to read a magazine, like a TV private eye.

Anna resists the impulse, because deep down she knows who the woman is. Not her name or face, but her job. Her profession. *Journo. She's with a tabloid, has to be.* Of course there are other people who might stalk Anna: relatives of Gavin's victims, or those low lifes the media flatters as vigilantes, but if the driver of the white Polo belonged in either of these categories she'd hardly sit there playing detective: she'd launch a physical assault or scream abuse. Or both.

Anna guesses what the journalist intends doing, it isn't hard. *The bitch means to follow me, find out where we live and tell the world. What can I do? If I start up, pull out of the queue, she'll either follow or wait at the Portsmouth terminal. She knows I have to leave the island sooner or later. I'm trapped.*

The boat's docked, vehicles are rolling ashore. Couple of minutes and the guy in the dayglo jacket'll beckon the queue to start boarding. Anna's mind's racing. *Six cars behind, she'll be ashore seconds after me and you can't put your foot down till you clear the dock area. Only chance would be if . . .*

An idea dawns as the queue starts moving. It's a scary idea, calling for the sort of behaviour she'd never dream of normally. *But this isn't a normal situation*, she tells herself, *I'll be doing it for Glen and Kayleigh, so they can rebuild their lives.*

Leaving the Polo on the car-deck, Anna joins the queue of passengers climbing the stairs to the bars and toilets, the open deck. She doesn't head for any of these facilities herself, but stands, inconspicuous in the throng, watching the stairs. She's relieved when her pursuer appears almost at once: if the journalist had decided for any reason to stay with her car, the plan would have had to be abandoned. As it is she hides her face till the woman passes from sight, waits till it seems nobody else is coming up and descends to the car-deck, praying there's no CCTV or, if there is, that nobody is watching the monitors.

She's lucky. No driver or passenger has stayed with a vehicle. If there's a crewman on the deck she doesn't encounter him. Cameras are nowhere in evidence, but she keeps her head bowed just in case.

One tyre's not enough, there'll be a spare wheel. She lets down both rear tyres, cringing at the noise the escaping air makes, hoping the journo won't notice till she's rolling, by which time Anna should be clear. Her heart's pounding, she's shaking and sweating but nothing's happened. Nobody's come. She can't believe she's done this, it's like she's somebody else, or in a play. It's a familiar sensation: she felt the same at Gavin's trial. She makes her way back to the stairs, unhurriedly, holding a handkerchief to her nose and mouth, and joins the queue for the toilet. Minutes pass. No hand falls on her shoulder. Nobody shows the slightest interest. As the queue shuffles patiently towards its goal, her heart rate slows to normal.

42

And she was definitely following you? asks Dad.

Mum nods. Oh, yes: why else would she have followed me to that dead-end village?

Hmm. He stares at the rug.

That means it could happen next time, I say flatly, or the time after. She can recognize you, knows you visit, all she has to do is wait.

Dad shakes his head. It might not be that bad, Glen. She can't know how long before the next visit, we don't know ourselves. She'd have to be there indefinitely and that costs money. I know these tabloids seem to have millions to splash around, but I can't see an editor keeping a member of staff on the Isle of Wight for weeks on end, waiting for your mother to show up. It could be months, they might even've transferred Gav to another prison and she wouldn't know.

Mum sighs. That's not the worry, there are other ways of tracing me. She could call DVLC with our car registration, ask for the address.

No. Dad shakes his head. They don't give out that sort of information, except to the police.

Mum shrugs. What about the ferry office then? They've got my details, credit-card number. All she has to do is ask.

Dad disagrees. They wouldn't tell her, Anna. He smiles briefly. If it were that easy we could all make a living as private detectives. No. He shakes his head again. I think it's important we don't get into a panic over this. What we need to do is work out a procedure for visits so that if somebody *does* follow, we don't lead 'em here. Couple of nights B and B might do the trick: one on the island, one on the mainland, something like that. He grins. She's a tabloid hack, how bright can she be?

DP, hi, it's Minnie.

'Bout time. Where're they skulking, eh?

Dunno, sir, she did my wheels.

Who? What d'you mean, *did my wheels*?

The mother. I spotted her at the prison, followed her on to the ferry.

And?

When we got to Portsmouth my back tyres were flat. Both of 'em. She'd let 'em down. They'd to tow me off, everybody behind me was livid and I'm stuck here overnight.

Brilliant, Minnie: you must've left it unattended.

Well of *course* I left it unattended: even *your* employees have to pee now and then. I wasn't gone more than fifteen minutes.

Long enough though. Found somewhere to stay, have you?

Yes.

Not Portsmouth's premier hotel, I trust. You've cost this paper a packet already for no result, but if you knock on my door at precisely three o'clock tomorrow afternoon and astound me with the brilliant idea you dreamed up overnight for locating this scumbag family, I might be merciful and sack you on the spot rather than have you dragged on to the roof and thrown off. Do I make myself quite clear, Minnie?

Clear as a bell, DP.

Splendid.

43

How'd it go last night? snoops Will as I leave the bike. My head's full of Mum's unhappy homecoming; don't know what he's referring to.

Huh?

Hangovers, you antibody: how'd you make out?

Hangovers . . . oh, couldn't make it in the end.

Chicken, eh?

No way, man. Something came up at home, you know how it is.

He nods. Tell me about it.

Watch the *Mystery of the Mummy's Curse*, did you?

Riddle of the Desert Mummies, yes.

What, no curse?

No. He's scornful. It was a scientific investigation not a horror movie, and they weren't the sort of mummies you're thinking of either. These were *natural* mummies: people who died in the desert and were never found till now. The sun dried out the corpses and the wind blew sand over 'em. The bacteria that normally make bodies decay can't function without moisture so they never rotted. You should've seen 'em: skin preserved, hair, nails. They can even tell what some of 'em *died* of. He grins. Quite a lot were murdered, but I don't suppose the police'll investigate: trail's bound to be a bit cold by now, even in the desert.

Not to mention the killer being three thousand years old, I add. I'm wishing the topic of murder hadn't come up, but I can't let Will see that.

Yeah! he laughs. What d'you give him, *life*?

The subject fizzles out after that except inside my head, where it messes with my mind for the rest of the day. I keep thinking how some guy 3,000 years ago murdered someone and buried the body in the desert. It wasn't found, which means he probably got away with it and enjoyed a much longer life than his victim, but we don't think of it like that. As far as we're concerned, they both lived and died 3,000 years ago and the fact that one killed the other doesn't matter at all, it's just interesting how the telltale signs have been preserved. So in 3,000 years' time, Gav and those women'll seem to have died at the same time, and if one of the bodies has been preserved so you can tell she was strangled, it'll be interesting rather than horrific. Time smooths everything out.

Trouble is, it takes time.

44

Then, just when you think you've filed it away in the recycle bin, something comes up to remind you. It's half-seven in the Crypt and I'm laying my woes on Rolf again.

He nods. That's how it tends to go, Glen, I'm afraid. What was it this time?

I tell him about my mummy conversation with Will. It was just a TV show about three-thousand-year-old mummies, Rolf. I was winding Will up a bit, calling it *Mystery of the Mummy's Curse*, and he started putting me right as I knew he would, and murder came up. I shrug. It was just a passing remark, but it's done my head in all day and that's what I mean: *everything* reminds you. It's like a conspiracy, you know: *let's make it impossible for Parish to have a normal day, even once in a while. Let's embed a glitch in every event, every conversation*. I shake my head. I don't think it'll ever leave me alone, Rolf. I can see these reminders popping up like that bloody paper clip in Word, even when I'm really old.

I'm nearly crying if you want to know. Rolf reaches across the table and squeezes my hand. It gets easier, Glen, believe me. He smiles. You said it yourself: *time smooths everything out*. It takes a while, but it happens eventually. All you can do in the meantime is tough it out.

We sip coffee, me with one eye on the stairs. I'm not convinced Will won't show up. Rolf notices, like he notices everything. Quit worrying, mate, he says. There's no lecture tonight, I checked. Your pal's on the sofa right now, watching *The Man Who Found Atlantis* on Beeb Two.

I look at him. Is there really something called that on Beeb Two tonight?

Oh, aye: you wait, he'll be full of it in the morning.

We get more coffees. I do my best to chill out. Rolf asks after Kayleigh and my parents. I tell him about Mum and the white Polo. He's really interested. Sounds like a tabloid all right, he says when I've finished. My dosh is on the *Post*: it's their style. He sighs. Danvers Pilkington, the self-righteous old hypocrite. Bangs on about the public's right to know, doesn't give a toss about the public. All he cares about is his law-and-order agenda and the circulation of his crappy paper. He'd have his mother kidnapped and posted home piece by piece in plastic bags if he thought it'd boost sales.

I nod. They're all the same, aren't they? One offered Virginia Mason's dad a hundred grand for an exclusive about his daughter's life and he actually *took* it. She's dead and he's rich, how sick is that?

Rolf shakes his head. Pretty sick.

I shiver. D'you think Danvers Pilkington'll find us, Rolf?

He pulls a face. I don't think so, Glen, not if your folks're careful over these visits. As your dad says, Pilkington won't keep a journo permanently on the island, and anyway, people'll get bored with Gavin Ward as soon as the next sensation comes along.

We sit till nine. Rolf's right about Will: he doesn't show, and the session's done me good as always. I even read a bit of *Wuthering Heights* before bed.

45

Morning, DP.

Oh so you're *back*, Minnie. Look, something's come up, I have to go out, powwow with those wimps at Advertising Standards. No time for your brilliant idea today, sweetheart.

Good, because there isn't one. Shall I clear my desk?

Clear your desk? The great man shakes his head. You don't get off *that* lightly, Minnie. Stick the Wards on the back burner, concentrate on this horse-bonking lark.

Horse bonking?

Don't tell me you haven't heard. Top trainer, stables in North Yorkshire, some sort of stallion costume. Caught on video, apparently.

Good grief, do the police know?

Not yet. The editor winks, grins. Enterprising stable maid came straight to us. Video's being checked for authenticity as we speak. I want you to get up there quick-sticks, talk to people: the man himself if he hasn't done a bunk. And not a word to anybody outside: this could be the biggest front page since the *Belgrano* and I want a *Post* exclusive. He leers, sketches a banner headline in the air: SILLY WILLIE'S WAY WITH FILLIES.

Minnie gasps. So it's . . .?

Willie Pegram, nods the editor. Allegedly.

Will finds me in the science block doorway. It's the first of October, drizzle blows across the yard. He combs wet hair with his fingers, mops his face with a Kleenex, sighs. No fun biking in this, Glen.

No, time to get the stretch limo out I reckon.

He grins. If only. Do anything thrilling last night?

Nah: Liam Gallagher dropped in, we wrote his next song.

Just the usual then, eh?

'S right.

Will smiles. There was a belting programme on Beeb Two.

Was there? *How d'you do it, Rolf?*

Oh yeah: *The Man Who Found Atlantis.*

Seen it. Harrison Ford, right?

No, not a movie: documentary. This American guy, professor, found these flat stones under the sea: sort of a pavement. Steps too, off the coast of Sicily.

Flat stones, uh? Pretty wild, wish I'd watched now.

He eyes me suspiciously. You're having me on again, aren't you?

Me: no.

Yes you are. You're not interested in anything intelligent.

I'm interested in Sally Prentice, she's intelligent.

Yeah, too intelligent to rate *you*, you blastocyst.

93

Hey watch it, we were *all* blastocysts once. Except Dennis Hawthorne, he started as a shellfish from Sainsbury's. His mum noticed it moving and put it in the fishtank, and it grew . . .

The buzzer interrupts this fantasy. Maybe if there'd been a buzzer in Emily Brontë's life, *Wuthering Heights*'d be shorter.

46

The amazing thing, goes Shikey, is that the spinster daughter of a clergyman, a girl who hardly ever left the isolated moorland village of her birth, who had virtually no experience with the opposite ah . . . sex, was able to come up with this very steamy novel of passion and revenge . . . What's funny, Baird?

Steamy, sir, smirks Baird. *I* haven't found nothing steamy in it; wish I had.

Shikey sighs. What you have to remember, lad, is that this book was published in the first half of the nineteenth century, a period when respectable women weren't supposed to write fiction of *any* sort, so a story by a curate's daughter about a wilful girl with the hots for a wild gypsy lad caused quite a scandal. Reviewers – all reviewers were men in those days – even insinuated that the author must be some sort of . . . er . . .

Slapper, sir? supplies Carla.

Well, yes, I suppose that's a rough equivalent, Carla.

Slag, says Hawthorne flatly. She were a slag, that's how come I don't rate her book.

No. Shikey shakes his head. The reason you don't rate *Wuthering Heights*, Hawthorne, is not that Emily Brontë is a slag, but that Dennis Hawthorne is a halfwit. *What* is Dennis Hawthorne?

Sir, a halfwit. He sounds quite proud.

So, resumes Shikey, rubbing his hands together, how did she manage it, eh? Where did all this scandalous stuff *come* from?

Sir, she could've got it off of the telly, suggests Wilson.

Shikey glowers at him. This isn't a clown competition, Wilson, I've asked a serious question.

Wilson looks nonplussed. I'm not joking, sir, a lot of people get ideas off of the telly. I know *I* do.

Shikey speaks softly, you can see the effort he's making not to bellow. *Wuthering Heights* was published in 1847, lad.

Wilson misses the significance. Sir?

Shikey looks as if he might cry. TV wasn't invented till the nineteen-thirties, Wilson: hardly anybody had it till the nineteen-fifties, by which time the Brontë sisters had been dead for about a hundred years.

The penny drops. Wilson looks downcast, then brightens. *I* know, sir: *videos*! When the telly's broke you watch videos, yeah?

You can see the intelligence shining in his eyes.

47

We're on edge for the next few days, more than usual. I catch myself keeping an eye open for white Polos, and it's amazing how many there are when you're looking for them. Mum didn't get a reg number, so any woman driving a white Polo is suspect. Twice, biking home, I spot white cars behind me and pull in till they pass. Will's with me both times, so I fake sneezing fits as an excuse to stop *and* to hide my face in a hanky. Neither driver shows the slightest interest and the second car isn't even a Polo, but it shows what a state I'm in and it must be the same for Mum and Dad.

Gav and I had this game when he used to take me with him in the truck. One of us'd nominate a model of car or other vehicle: a Yaris, say, or a Passat, or one of Eddie Stobart's trucks, and there'd be a point for whoever spotted one first as we hummed along. I suppose it was just a way of passing the time for him, but I used to really enjoy it, not least because it was the only game where I had a chance of beating him: he always slaughtered me at bowling. I don't . . . *slaughtered*'s the wrong word, I wasn't thinking, but you know what I mean.

Anyway she doesn't show up and bit by bit we relax. Halfway through October the weather turns nasty. We're halfway through *Wuthering Heights* in Shikey's class, and it feels sort of *right* to be ploughing through it while a blustery wind flings rain at the classroom window. I keep hoping something'll happen to make him cancel the Haworth expedition, but nothing does, and when the deadline rolls round I bring in the dosh like everybody else.

Which brings us to Hallowe'en. Not that I celebrate Hallowe'en in any way: I grew out of that years ago, but something happens this time that makes it unforgettable, at least for Mum and Kayleigh.

Kayleigh's the reason we've been aware of Hallowe'en approaching. They've been doing all the usual stuff at Highfield Primary: cutting out witches on broomsticks from black paper and sticking them on to the classroom windows, silhouetted against big yellow moons which echo the row of fat orange pumpkins on the sill. She's brought home her collage of witches dancing round a cauldron, with flames of red and orange foil and a black cat perched on its rim. Myself, I'm a bit uneasy about Hallowe'en this year. I couldn't say why exactly, but I suppose it's to do with Gav and the stuff he did, same as everything else. Mum pins Kayleigh's collage to the fridge with magnets, but she's uneasy as well, I can see it in her eyes.

Anyway, the evening itself rolls round, and we're watching telly with the fire on and the curtains drawn. Kayleigh's sulking a bit because Stephanie's out trick or treating with girls from school and she wants to go too. Mum's forbidden this without offering an answer to the child's plaintive, *Why*, Mum, why *can't* I?

I know why she doesn't want her out there in the dark,

and it isn't hard to understand why she won't explain. She *can't*, because what reason would she give? Same one every mother gives of course: *it's not safe, sweetheart, there are men, funny men . . .*

Go figure.

For a time it seems the trick or treaters are avoiding our house, but just after eight comes the anticipated knock. Dad's brought some stuff home from Caffyn's: little black bags with jack-o'-lanterns on them and a handful of sweets inside. Mum scoops up a few of these and heads for the door, taking Kayleigh with her. Dad and I gawp on.

We're aware of the door being opened. Childish squeals ought to follow, but they don't. What follows is a drawn-out, terrified scream from Mum. Before it even stops we're up, getting under each other's feet as we charge out to the hallway. Mum's trying to close the door but she's hobbled by Kayleigh clinging to her skirt. They're both shrieking. On the step, shocked into paralysis by the effect their costumes have produced, stand the phosphorescent skeletons of five girls.

Dad susses the situation at once, and I'm not far behind. He scoops up Kayleigh and flings his free arm round Mum, hugging and shushing.

I pick the bags off the floor and hold them out to the girls who're backing off, stuttering apologies. Here, take 'em, I soothe. It's all right, it's not your fault, my mum's . . .

They mumble, shake their luminous skulls and hurry away as fast as their preposterous platform shoes will allow. I'm left on the step, with the treats in my hands and my family in a moaning clump at my back.

Happy Hallowe'en.

48

Rolf says I should check out Young Teens night at Hangovers: reckons I'm in danger of becoming a recluse. I was a bit late for our appointment last Wednesday, and I made the mistake of telling him I don't like these dark evenings.

Why? he asks.

I say I don't know. I *do* know, sort of, but it's too vague to put into words. He keeps on at me though, and in the end I tell him how Mum looked at me funny when I went out on Bonfire Night.

He frowns. What d'you mean, *funny*?

Oh, you know: like she was wondering what I was going to be doing out there.

He shrugs, smiles. She probably *was*, Glen: kids get up to all sorts on Bonfire Night.

I shake my head. It wasn't like that. She was thinking about girls, I know she was. Me and girls.

You and girls?

Yeah. She's worried I might be like Gav.

Is she, Glen? He looks at me intently. Are you sure it's your mum and not *you* who's worried about that?

I can't stand it when he starts in on the psychological

bullshit, I get mad. It's *both* of us, I snarl. But I can fight it in me, I can't fight it in her. It's easier just to stay home; I nearly didn't come tonight.

And that's it. That's when he comes out with the recluse bit: tells me I'll end up a prisoner in my own home if I don't make the effort and get out more.

So it's seven o'clock Tuesday, pitch-black outside, and here I am in my coolest kit, hot to boogie. I take a last look at my gorgeous self in the mirror and head for the stairs.

Aren't you taking a coat, love? goes Mum in the kitchen. There's a cold wind.

I shake my head. I don't have dosh for the cloakroom, Mum.

Then why don't I run you down there in the car, it's only five minutes?

Make sure I go where I say I'm going, you mean. It's all right, Mum, I'll be fine.

Are you meeting somebody, is that it?

No, I'm not meeting anybody. *Not stalking anybody either.* I'm walking, by myself.

What time do you expect to be home?

I shrug. Place shuts at eleven, Tuesdays. Should be in a few minutes after, depending how the taxis are.

Your dad could come for you, he wouldn't mind.

You don't get it do you, Mum? I have to do this myself. No need, Mum, it'll be fine.

I shiver, walking down the path, and it isn't just the cold.

49

I clubbed a few times, back in my Dale Ward days. Moby Disc the place was called, and Hangovers is very similar: house music, fast and loud, subdued lighting, packed floor. I head for the gents' where I slip the light sticks inside my shoes and activate the panel. All the mirrors have kids in front of them, fussing with their hair. I don't get to see how I look but I don't need to, I know I look terrific.

I stroll to the bar, get a Doctor Pepper and scan the dancers for faces I know. There are plenty. I see Victor Gott and Clinton Quinn, Lynn Jarvis and Tracey Popplewell and Lucy Baxter. Lucy wears her glittery pants so low it's a wonder they stay up, and Lynn's in a see-through top. Watching them starts me aching in unusual places, but I'm not grumbling and anyway, the second I spot Sally Prentice everything else is wiped.

She's absolutely drop-dead gorgeous. I mean she's gorgeous at *school*, but that's nothing, *nothing* compared with the way she's looking now. She's wearing a clingy crop top under a short, sleeveless jacket, skimpy running shorts, high boots with pointy toes and a baseball cap with *Lady* across the front. Everything's in pale mauve except the boots, which are black. It's amazing her parents let her leave the house like that. I gawp, I sigh, my teeth feel soft. I'm melting into my trainers.

I could eat chips out of her knickers, said a guy in a movie I once saw. Gazing at Sally I know exactly what he meant, only there'd be very few chips in this portion. She's glancing about, seeing who's here. I lift a hand but her eyes sweep past like I'm invisible. Distress plucks at my guts, but before it can get a hold she does the sort of double take you only get in animations and looks straight at me.

I can hardly believe it's me who's caught her attention. I even check behind in case Blue's Duncan is there, but it's definitely me. She sashays across. Glen, she says. Cool kit. I didn't know you . . .

You didn't *know* me? I croak.

No. She smiles, shakes her head. I was going to say I didn't know you had gear like this. You hang out with the Willie, I just assumed your stuff'd be like his.

Hell no. I lift a shoe that pulsates with green light. They won't let you in the institute wearing these, they'd distract the lecturer.

She nods. Distracted *me*. We dancing or what?

So then I'm dancing with scrummy Sally Prentice. *Me*. It's like a dream. Carla's here as well, sharing herself between Clinton, who likes it if you call him Clint, and Victor, who hates Vic. The number ends, another starts, the dream goes on. Rolf's right as usual: this is easily the highest I've been since Gav's arrest.

You get shattered though. It's hot and the floor's packed, and after a bit you're sweating like a pig. There's no way I'm going to call time out, not with Sally moving and smiling in front of me. In the end it's her who shakes her head ruefully and shouts in my ear, chill-out room, yeah?

She tells Carla, and the three of us make our way over there. Clint and Vic have gone to the bar. In the chill-out room every table's taken. I don't mind standing if Sally'll stay and chat, but Carla spots some empty seats and leads us to them. Mind if we join you? she asks the three lads round the table.

One looks up, shrugs. We don't give a stuff, do we lads? says Hawthorne.

50

I sit down right next to him to show I'm not bothered either. He glances at me sidelong, edges away a bit, looks across at Sally. Don't say you're with this weirdo, Sal.

It's *Sally*, she corrects, and yes, I am as a matter of fact.

Why?

Sally shrugs. He's got cooler stuff than you, *and* he can read.

I could've hugged her. Hawthorne has no comeback, Baird and Wilson snigger in their drinks.

Clint and Vic appear with Cokes for the girls. Sally takes hers, looks at Gott. What about Glen?

What about him?

You haven't bought him a drink.

Gott looks scandalized. Why the heck should I, he's not a mate of mine.

No, smiles Sally, but he's a mate of *mine*. And besides, it's not polite to leave somebody out.

I stand up. It's OK, Sally, I can get my own. *I've enough enemies, don't make me another.*

No! She shakes her head, motions me to sit. Victor's getting you one, aren't you, *darling*?

What d'you want? grunts Gott, avoiding my eyes.

Doctor Pepper, I tell him. Please. He goes off. Quinn stands by the table with his drink; there isn't a seat for him. We sip while Gary Numan sings 'Cars'.

Everything that's happened since Sally did that double take seems unreal to me. A few hours ago her eyes mocked me across the classroom, now she's got an alpha male buying my drink. I suppose alarm bells should be ringing, but they're not. They're not. I'm besotted, can't tear my eyes away from her angel's face.

Angel. That's a laugh if ever there was one. She sits there and smiles for me, only for me, and all the time she's engineering my fall.

The guys' drinks are getting low. Rapt on that pale mauve outfit and the little it conceals, I don't notice till she leans across and covers my hand with hers. I think it might be your turn to get the Cokes, she murmurs.

Oh . . . oh yeah. I leap up, so eager to please it's pathetic. I take everybody's order, praying I've got the dosh to cover it. The dance floor's more crowded than ever, and it's murder getting served at the bar. Eventually I catch the barman's eye, stump up nearly every penny I've got and carry the tray to the chill-out room.

Gott's in my seat. Hawthorne's swapped places with Sally and she's snuggled up to Victor, who has his arm round her. I force myself to hand out the glasses as if nothing's wrong, though I've gone hot and my heart's pounding. When everybody's served I have to say something. I look at Sally.

W-What's happening?

How d'you mean? The mockery's back in those wide eyes.

Why've you moved? Why's his arm round you? You were with me.

With *you*? She snorts. I don't think so.

You said I was a mate of yours. It sounds pathetic, even to me.

Did I? Her eyes widen further. I don't remember.

Hey, Parish, goes Hawthorne. Why don't you take your e-shirt and your poxy glow shoes and go piss up a dolmen? Everybody cracks out laughing. People're turning to see what's funny and it's me, *I'm* funny.

And I lose it. *You*'d've lost it in my place, don't say you wouldn't. I throw myself across the table and drive my fist into Gott's face as hard as I possibly can. He goes over backwards, clutching his spurting nose. Off balance I sprawl on the table, which tips. An avalanche of glasses slides to the floor and I follow, crushing tumblers under me as I land on the soggy carpet.

Hurt, but high on hate, I start to get up. All I want is to mash Gott's silly face so he'll never laugh again, but when I try to make a fist I can't, there's something wrong with my hand. The guys're holding me back anyway, pinning me down, shouting at me to leave it. They're trying to save me from the doormen, but I don't realize that till a pair of them arrive at the double, grabbing fistfuls of my expensive kit, jerking me to my feet. Before I know what's happening they're giving me the bum's rush, out of the chill-out room, straight across the dance floor and down the stairs to the exit. While one of them opens the door, his mate plants his foot on my arse and sends me flying like a rag doll to the pavement. The door slams shut. I lie bewildered on my back as drizzle drifts down on my face and the soles of my shoes illuminate the wet flagstones intermittently with a green, pulsating glow.

51

Mother, it's Anna. Are you all right?

Anna, your voice sounds queer, what's up?

Bit of a cold, that's all. I'm calling because you haven't replied to my last two letters.

I *have*, I posted one the day before yesterday, first class. And one about a fortnight ago.

Oh . . .

Didn't you get them?

No. I *thought* it was a bit odd: wondered if you were ill or something.

No, dear, I'm absolutely fine. I can't understand it, it's been all right up to now.

Are you using the postcode, Mother?

Of course I am, Anna: always have. And why *Mother* all of a sudden: what's wrong with Mum?

Nothing's wrong with it, Mum: I'm starting to speak like the people here, I suppose. Listen.

What?

Have you got the postcode written down somewhere?

Yes, in my address book. Why?

D'you think you could've copied it down wrong?

I don't think so, dear, or my earlier letters would've gone astray too.

Will you check, Mum, now, while I hold on: just to be on the safe side?

Yes, dear, of course I will. But I've a question for you first.

What is it, Mum?

What was your dad's nickname for you, when you were a little girl?

Mu-um: what's *that* got to do with anything? I don't remember anyway.

Well that's strange, considering he's never called you anything else. Who *are* you: a reporter?

Blast!

Hello . . .?

52

I get up when the wet's soaked through my tee and baggies and I'm freezing. My hoodie's in Hangovers' cloakroom; I'm not up for trying to retrieve it tonight. That round of drinks has left me two quid short of a taxi fare and the battery's down on my phone, so I'm walking. I've made a complete prat of myself, or rather I've let Sally Prentice do it for me, in front of all the school dons, and there's a nasty cut across my right palm from falling on broken glass. As somebody or other once said, I've had a wonderful evening, but this wasn't it.

Worse to come at home. Twenty to twelve I stagger in and Mum's waited up, twitchy as hell. When she sees the state of me she's like, What's happened, Glen? What have you done?

Done? I screech, I haven't *done* anything, Mum: stuff's been done *to* me. I know exactly what's been going through her mind while she's paced about waiting and I shouldn't yell at her, but the whole thing's doing my head in and I can't help it. I'm not *him*, I shout, I'm *me*. I act like a prat, lose half my kit and mop the street with what's left and I don't get the girl, but I don't throttle her either.

I'm well out of order and I know it. Mum bursts into tears, Dad comes down in his pyjamas and starts giving me a right bollocking, and in the middle of it all we find Kayleigh on the stairs looking haunted.

I simmer down, apologize. Mum notices my hand and attends to it. Dad takes my sister back to her bed and returns to his own. Mum and I go up together. On the landing she murmurs, Goodnight, son, and gives me a peck on the cheek, which she hasn't done in years.

In my room I shuck off the fancy kit and chuck it in a corner, for all the good it's done me.

I'm crying if you must know, and it's not Sally Prentice: it's my sister's pasty face and that peck on the cheek. And Gav in his narrow bed, pasty-faced too and kissed by nobody.

53

I wake to the rattle of rain on my window, the booming of wind round the house. It's Wednesday, the morning after the night before and I really really don't want to go to school. I lie staring at the ceiling while a video of last night's disaster plays inside my skull. I'm trying not to watch it: I need a foolproof excuse for staying home so I should concentrate on that.

Mum, I don't feel well.

Mum, the bike-lock key's in my hoodie and my hoodie's down Hangovers.

Mum, Shikey Fenton says I've been working too hard, I need complete rest.

Mum, I lied to you. I wasn't at Hangovers last night.

I was abducted by aliens, medically examined on board their ship. I think I have an implant.

Yeah, right.

Mum's doing toast. No sign of Dad or Kayleigh. Morning, Mum, where're Dad and Kayleigh?

Morning, Glen. She looks strained. Dad's on lates, he's having a lie-in. And Kayleigh had a disturbed night, wet the bed. I'm keeping her home.

I could stay too if you like, look after her. Don't go there, don't even think about it.

Sorry, Mum: it's my fault isn't it?

She smiles tiredly. It's everybody's fault, love, and nobody's. We're victims of our situation, the four of us. I half expected . . .

What?

Nothing, Glen: it didn't happen so it doesn't matter. Your gran phoned last night.

Yeah? Any news?

Mum pulls a face. Sort of. Not good I'm afraid. Somebody called her. Some woman, pretending to be me.

What the heck *for*? Gran'd know it wasn't you anyway.

She tried to disguise her voice, said she had a cold. Gran got suspicious when the sneaky witch tried to get her to read out our postcode. Mum smiles briefly. So she asked her a simple question: what was Grandad's nickname for me when I was little. And, of course, she hadn't a clue.

She could've had a stab at it, like the guy in *Rumpelstiltskin.*

Yes, and with about the same chance of success. Who calls a kid *Pookie*, for goodness' sake?

So what happened?

Mum shrugs. She said *blast* and hung up.

And who *was* she, d'you think?

Reporter I guess: the one in the white Polo. If your gran hadn't sussed her she'd have our postcode; she'd've been here today, blowing our cover. It's terrifying.

It doesn't make me feel any better, I can tell you. Doesn't even translate into a day off for me.

It's still pissing down so Mum drives me. Means catching the bus home, Dad'll have the car, but before that I've got to survive six hours of total humiliation.

Can't wait.

54

I don't have to: they're loitering by the gate. Quinn, Gott, Hawthorne, Wilson and Baird. Gott's bruised eyes are linked by a cut across the bridge of his nose. As Mum pulls away in the Polo he tosses something towards me. My catch is a reflex action, it's my hoodie. Thought you might want it, he growls. I look from the garment to him, my brain can't reconcile his wounds and his thoughtfulness till I notice they're all smirking and there's a bad smell. I hold up the top and look at it. They've buttered the hood and pockets with dog muck, the dirty pigs.

Pop it on, suggests Hawthorne. Have another shot at Sally: if that flaky e-shirt turned her on she's *bound* to go for a state-of-the-art, scratch-and-sniff doggy-bog top.

Too nauseated to speak, I fling the garment down and head for the washroom. If I scrub my hands and take some sips of cold water I might keep from throwing up. Their jeers follow me, and I see Sally and Carla watching from their spot by the staffroom window.

I get through it. You have to, don't you? It's a long day though, avoiding eye contact with my tormentors, trying to convince myself Sally Prentice is an ugly slag I never really fancied. Long day.

Crafty cow, goes Rolf when I tell him about the phone call to Gran. We're at our usual table, it's sleeting outside, there's more staff than customers.

I nod gloomily. I know, makes you wonder whether there's any point in all this *Being John Malkovitch* stuff. I mean, they're gonna track us down sooner or later, aren't they?

He shakes his head. Not necessarily, Glen. He grins briefly. Especially if they keep coming up against people as sharp as your gran.

I've already laid the sad saga of Hangovers and the hoodie on him. I don't know how he stands it, listening to depressed fokkers like me day after day and having to come up with positive responses. I tell him it's a wonder he doesn't top himself and he shakes his head.

What my clients need most is someone to listen, so I listen, and the stuff I hear convinces me I'm the luckiest guy I know, so the therapy works both ways. He shrugs. You're helping me as much as I'm helping you, Glen.

We get refills and I help him a bit more by telling him

how worried I am now the Haworth trip's looming. He thinks I should go, but then he thought I should go to Hangovers and look how *that* turned out.

Good to talk though.

55

There are no pictures of Gav in our front room. There's Mum and Dad's wedding photo, school shots of me and Kayleigh and a black-and-white of Gran. It's the same with the family albums: all shots that included my brother were removed and burned at the bottom of the garden the day after we moved here. Mum and Dad think the house is free of them but it isn't. Not quite.

Well it's a sort of betrayal, isn't it, sending a family member to the recycle bin so it's like he never existed? They even burned his baby pics.

I rescued him though. I saved the best shot. It's an enlargement of a snap taken at Flamingoland on his birthday, the day I told you about. He's standing on a path, shielding his eyes from the sun, grinning at the camera. He looks so happy you'd never guess he'd rather be bowling. If they'd printed *this* in the papers instead of the police mugshot they always use, at least people'd see he's a guy and not some monster.

Nobody knows I've got it. I took it out of its frame and stuck it to the back of my Mis-Teeq poster with Blu-tack, and sometimes at night I peel it off and look at it and I'll tell you this: whoever said the camera never lies was talking a load of old bollocks.

56

Isn't November a crap month? Dark mornings, dark again by teatime. Cold, wet and windy, with five months of the same to look forward to. It's as if the atmosphere of *Wuthering Heights* has leaked out and polluted the whole environment, like GM rape.

Everywhere's tinselled up already, which is daft because it means people're sick of Christmas before it comes. It's like starting with witches and broomsticks and jack-o'-lanterns first week in September. We might as well just leave the decorations up all year and have Christmas and Hallowe'en all the time.

It's me, of course. Everything's getting on top of me in spite of Rolf's best efforts. He says Mum's not watching me but how does he know, he doesn't live at our house. She hates it when I go out after dark, and if I'm a bit late back she's strung out like someone waiting for a fix. Dad's probably the same, though he doesn't show it as much. It's bad enough coping with parental expectation when it's all about grades and qualifications: nightmare when you know they're half expecting you to start strangling people. Then there's the feeling of being hunted. That never goes away. Just when you think your camouflage is starting to match the background, along comes a woman in a white Polo to start you sweating again. And on top of that there's the Haworth trip, where I get to choose between going and probably bumping into 600 people who know I'm Dale Ward, and drawing attention to myself by chickening out.

But the worst things of all are the things that go on in my head. I mean, the way Mum watches me is *nothing* compared to the way I watch myself. Imagine having to analyse every action, decision, feeling: every thought, looking for first signs, without knowing what the signs *are*. I mean Gav never acted strange, but surely there must've been *something*: something Mum and Dad might've picked up on if they'd known what to look for: if they'd known there was reason to look.

He was keen on bowling, but if *that*'s one of the signs there're an awful lot of psychopaths out there. I'd love to believe it *was* a telltale sign, because I can take bowling or leave it. He never had a regular girlfriend, but lots of guys don't: doesn't mean they want to throttle women. He enjoyed driving, but so does Jacques Villeneuve. And he was always good with me and Kayleigh.

So, I'm watching myself every minute of every day, but I don't know what I'm looking for. Could the urge to analyse everything you do be a sign in itself?

You can probably imagine how screwed up I am. I sit on my bed looking at my brother's photo, and I can't cry for him like I used to. Is *that* a sign? The last thing I want is to start blaming Gav for everything, but it does all stem from what he did, doesn't it? And it isn't fair, because I haven't done anything. I haven't done anything and I'm forced to live like this, with a false name at a rotten school in a strange town. And it's going to be like this forever.

I'm doing life, for nothing.

57

The month wears on. The Mafia seem to have got bored roughing me up, though they give me plenty of verbal, which I do my best to ignore. I've still got the hots for Sally. She knows it, and acts like I'm not there. Mum manages to get most of the muck off my top and it goes to the cleaner's, but then it just hangs in my wardrobe with the rest of my kit. I've no plans to revisit Hangovers. Will's gone into winter mode: I imagine him spending his evenings and weekends cataloguing his collection of dolmen snaps or writing jokes for Roger Fenby or whatever. At any rate he stays home, and *my* only outings are Wednesdays to see Rolf.

We finish reading *Wuthering Heights*. Shikey's promised us a GCSE-style exam on it before Christmas, so that's something to look forward to. In the meantime we're supposed to start re-reading it so it'll stay fresh in our minds but *I'm* not: I'd rather shove burning splinters under my fingernails.

December blows in on a blast of wind and sleet.

Nothing horrible's come out of Mum's encounter with the girl in the white Polo, so during the first week of the month she risks another visit. She's careful as hell, but sees no sign of anyone watching or following. She comes back upset, having delivered our pathetic Chrissy presents to Gav. This'll be the first Christmas since my sister was born we haven't been together, and *of course* we think about the families of those poor murdered women and it doesn't help at all, it makes it infinitely worse.

And I suppose it's because we seem to have shaken off the vultures that Mum and Dad let Rolf talk them into packing me off to Haworth with my classmates. I don't want to go, I'd much rather chuck a sickie, but they gang up on me, saying if I don't go I'll draw attention to myself. Load of old bollocks if you ask me, but still.

The fateful day dawns dull and drizzly, so numerous jokey references to wuthering are inevitable as we clamber aboard our luxury coach in the schoolyard. My plan to sit as near Sally as possible is scuppered when Shikey and Emma steer girls to one side of the aisle, boys to the other like they were never young themselves.

And have you noticed how every coach driver is a clone of Adolf Hitler? Ours goes on for at least ten minutes about staying in our seats, not putting chewing gum in the ashtrays and using the toilet only when absolutely necessary. Why the heck do they bother putting toilets on coaches if you can't use them? We mustn't upset people by gurning or mooning out of the windows, we're not to distract the driver and blaa blaa blaa blaa blaa. It goes on so long I start wondering if we're actually off anywhere, or has old Waggy bought this coach as an extra class-room. It's ten past nine when the guy stops the rabbit and starts the bus. I've no way of knowing it, but this excursion's going to change everything in my life.

Again.

58

A good way to make 200 miles feel like a thousand is to sit next to Will Tomlinson. As we rumble north I hear everything there is to hear about his camera, his laptop, his collection of forties' hits on CD and the system he's devised for filing newspaper clippings according to interest level, rather than alphabetically or chronologically. I fall asleep crossing Derbyshire, and wake up as Hitler wrenches the coach into a split-ass turn through the gateway of Langlands Youth Hostel at Haworth.

It's raining. At first glance, the hostel looks like one of those places travellers spend the night at in vampire movies. You can tell by just looking that something horrible's bound to happen there, and you wonder why the travellers don't sense it too and drive on.

It's OK inside though. The warden, a comfy woman called Beth with frizzy hair and glasses, explains the rules and shows us the dormitories. At this point a fantasy I've cultivated for a week or so, involving a complicated mix-up over sleeping arrangements which leaves me and Sally Prentice sharing a cosy room under the rafters, withers and fades away. The girls' dormitory is in the east wing of the house, the boys' is in the west. Each has its own bathrooms and toilets. The only shared areas are a lecture room and the refectory, both downstairs.

Ah, well.

It's three o'clock, it'll be dark soon, so we don't go out. Instead we pile into the lecture room where a local historian tells us what Haworth was like in the Brontës' time. I've heard it all before: the open sewer; the drinking water that came via the graveyard; the epidemics; the life expectancy of twenty-six years – eighteen if you were a woolcomber; the babies killed by laudanum. I doze with my mind in free fall, constructing a scenario in which me and Sally get accidentally locked inside the parsonage tomorrow night. Sally's so scared she lets me cuddle her on the sofa till morning, and naturally I don't tell her Emily died on it.

And so to bed, as Samuel Pepys used to say. It's bunks, and I've bagged a top one with Will underneath. A mistake as it turns out. One of the rules is lights out at ten, but Will's brought a torch. He's the sort of guy who if you were off down Sainsbury's to buy cornflakes, he'd bring a torch. He jiggles about for ages, sorting out his notes from the lecture. We weren't even meant to *take* notes, but he keeps me awake till eleven at the earliest. Still, this is nothing compared to what'll have me lying awake tomorrow night, and it won't be Emily's horsehair sofa.

59

Well now. Shikey rubs his hands together to generate enthusiasm while Emma beams beside him. Twenty sceptical faces gaze back at them. Breakfast over, we're in the lecture room to hear how we'll spend our day.

It's half past eight. Rain lashes the window. Bit of wuthering, sir, offers Hawthorne.

Shikey sighs. *Somebody* had to say it I suppose, Hawthorne: it might as well be you. However. He brightens. The weather need not concern us, since we will spend this morning inside the famous parsonage. What's it famous *for*, Wilson?

Uh . . . Heathcliff lived there, sir. And Cathy.

Dunderhead, groans Shikey as the rest of us titter. He glowers at Wilson. Why do I waste my life, lad, eh? Why do I waste my life in futile attempts to get through to prehistoric life forms such as yourself?

Dunno, sir.

No, and neither do I. He turns to me. Tell him, Parish: tell him why neither Heathcliff nor Cathy Earnshaw ever set foot inside Haworth parsonage, or anywhere else for that matter.

Sir, because they're fictional characters. I speak sullenly, so he'll know I don't want to be teacher's pet.

Shikey nods. Because they're fictional characters. Thank

you, Parish. He turns back to Wilson. Let me know when that reaches your brain, will you?

It *has*, sir.

What, already? You must be evolving, Wilson, before our very eyes. Know what *that* means I suppose: evolving?

Yes, sir: going round and round.

Shikey winces. Gradual process, evolution, he murmurs. Mustn't rush it. He glances at Emma Royd, she's giggling like a twelve-year-old, like he's the wittiest thing since Groucho Marx. He's lapping it up as well: playing the whole scene for her benefit. Wouldn't surprise me if . . .

He smiles briefly in my direction. Handy to have a local expert on board, Parish. I shrug, my eyes on the floor. Hawthorne mutters something I don't catch. Shikey proceeds to tell us what Haworth parsonage is actually famous for, spinning it out, probably hoping the rain'll stop.

I did the parsonage about four times when we lived up here. It's a museum, with rooms made to look as they would have in the Brontë era. It's OK the first time, but five's four too many if you know what I mean. I have to do it though, and at least Shikey doesn't pull that local expert stunt again, which is a relief. It takes us about forty minutes to go round, and everybody's pretty bored except Will and the teachers. Will's brought his notebook. He reads all the placards from start to finish and copies out the best bits while we all wait for him. The kids hate this, and it's worse for me because I'm scared somebody on the staff might recognize me. All I want to do is get the visit over and be out in the rain so I can hunch into my coat collar and keep my head down.

You exit through a shop, same as most museums. Some of the kids want to get stuff for their mums, which takes a while. The old girl behind the counter looks familiar so I stand in a corner with my back to everyone, pretending to be fascinated by some glazed busts of Charlotte which flatter her outrageously, the real Charlotte having been more than ordinarily plain. Because of the weather we hadn't left the hostel till after ten, so it's nearly twelve when we finally get out of the shop.

Shikey's original plan was to take us straight from the parsonage up to Top Withens, a ruined farmhouse on the moor which is supposed to have inspired *Wuthering Heights*. We've brought packed lunches, but it's three miles each way and the rain's sheeting. He gathers us on the gleaming cobbles.

Change of plan. He juts his underlip and blows a droplet off the end of his nose. Miss Royd has phoned Beth and it's OK for us to go back and eat our packed lunches at the hostel. He pulls a rueful face. Pity, but it can't be helped. Better forecast for tomorrow apparently: colder but mostly dry, so we'll leave Top Withens till then.

We trudge through the village, me with my baseball cap well down and my face in my collar. We're nearly there when Royd, who's leading, stops us and calls to Shikey bringing up the rear. Mr Fenton, there's a lollipop lady just ahead. We might as well cross with her, mightn't we?

Good idea, Miss Royd, enthuses Shikey, as though

she's discovered penicillin. Cross with the lady, folks, he commands.

My heart kicks me in the ribs. I know the lady, and what's more she knows me. Sugden's her name. Mrs Sugden: me and Gav used to cross with her all the time. She'll recognize me for sure. For a split second I consider crossing here, before we reach her, but then I see what'll happen. Shikey'll spot me and bellow. I'll have to stop, even if I've reached the other side. He'll make me come back and cross with everybody else, and I'll be the centre of attention. Mrs Sugden's attention. No. All I can do is keep my head down and hope she won't notice.

I work my way into the thick of the group at the kerb. Sugden's a metre away. I stare at the ground. Two cars swish by, then she raises her lollipop and steps out. I cross, holding my breath, keeping Kim Baird between myself and the lady. My scalp prickles in anticipation of the cry that'll blow my cover, ruin my life.

It doesn't come. *It doesn't come.* I'm on the pavement in a ruck of my fellow pupils, walking away and it's all right. She hasn't spotted me and she won't now, she can only see my back. I exhale, feeling light as air. I was a metre away and I wasn't recognized, so maybe Rolf was right. He said people soon forget, move on to the next sensation. Maybe it's happened already: the Wards're forgotten, something's taken their place.

Hey, Parish, you lymphocyte. Hawthorne's voice, he's right behind. What's that lolly-waving grave dodger got against you, eh?

My heart kicks again. Why, what d'you mean?

Ha! You should've seen her face when she looked at you, like you strangled her budgie or something. *Did* you strangle her budgie, Parish? Is that why you had to move away?

60

Bromley 646282, Minnie Cooper here.

Hello? Is this MOVE ON?

MOVE ON? I think you must have the wrong ... who's speaking?

My name's Mrs Sugden, I was hoping to speak to Veronica Craven. She gave me a card with this number on it.

Oh, I see what's happened. This is Veronica's *home*, she gave you her home number. MOVE ON's a different number altogether.

Oh, I'm sorry, I didn't know. Is Miss Craven there, by any chance?

You're lucky, Mrs Sugden. She wouldn't normally be at home during office hours, but it so happens she's down with a sore throat today. If you'd like to hold I'll call her.

Oh, I don't think we should bother her if she's ill, Miss er ...

Cooper. Veronica's not ill, Mrs Sugden, it's just her throat. One moment please.

Veronica Craven here, how may I help you?

Ooh, you do sound *hoarse*, Miss Craven. This is Mrs Sugden: you know, the lollipop lady you spoke to in . . .

Yes, I remember, you were most helpful. What can I do for you?

I thought you'd be interested to know the brother's here with a school party.

Brother?

Yes, Dale Ward, Gavin's brother.

Is he? How d'you know this, Mrs Sugden?

I saw him with my own eyes, not more than an hour ago. Whole party crossed with me, two teachers.

And you're *sure* it was Dale Ward? You couldn't be mistaken?

Course I'm sure, he was that near I could've reached out and touched him. *If* I didn't mind soiling my fingers, I mean.

Yes, quite. You don't happen to know whereabouts in the country this party's from, I suppose?

No, I don't. Somewhere down south, judging by their accents. They were going towards Langlands.

What's Langlands?

Youth hostel. School parties stay there a lot.

Well, that *is* interesting. Thank you so much for taking the trouble to call, Mrs Sugden: our work at MOVE ON would be a great deal more difficult if it weren't for the kind cooperation of people like yourself.

Oh, it's nothing, Miss Craven: not if it helps the families of those poor murdered girls. Goodbye, and I hope you'll be feeling better soon.

Oh I *will*, Mrs Sugden, believe me.

61

You're talking shite, man. Why would she be giving *me* dirty looks, she doesn't know me from Adam.

Hawthorne shrugs. You'd have to ask her, but it was definitely you she was looking at. I reckon she was your girlfriend – some guys go for the older woman – and you ditched her when you moved south.

The kids're laughing as we trudge through the rain. I'm not. *Strangled her budgie.* Why strangled? Why not squashed or shot or poisoned? And girlfriend. He's just horsing around, I know, but why those particular words? And if she *has* recognized me, what will she do? Tell people? Get a mob together? Am I going to wake up in the middle of the night to find Langlands surrounded by vigilantes baying for my blood?

And what can I *do* about it: collar Shikey, tell him his trip's crap dot com and I'm off home? Course not. Sneak away, catch a train? That'd get me out of Haworth, but not out of trouble. No. All I can do is sit tight and hope nothing happens. And join in the banter to deflect suspicion, though I never felt less like joshing.

You got it second try, Dennis.

Huh?

There was no budgie but we *were* an item, Lolly and me. That was my special name for her by the way: Lolly. I couldn't take her clubbing, they'd think she was the cleaner, so we used to sit in teashops, talk about knitting and varicose veins. Oh, and sometimes we'd go to the pictures, watch old comedies with Doris Day.

It works. By the time we arrive back at the hostel they're laughing with me, not at me, but I'm not a happy bunny all the same. Hawthorne wasn't mistaken: course he wasn't. Old Sugden spotted me for sure. Question is, will she do anything about it?

It's a question only time will answer, and I know I'm in for another restless night.

62

Morning, DP: it's Minnie.

Ah, Minnie. Superb job on the Willie Pegram thing: well done.

Thanks. I'm off to Yorkshire again actually, that's what I called to tell you.

Why, what's happening?

I've had a tip-off, DP. Gavin Ward's brother's surfaced. He's at Haworth with a school party.

Is he by jove?

Yes, so I thought I'd drive up there first thing tomorrow, get the name of the school and where it is. Once we know that, finding the family'll be a doddle.

D'you know where the party's staying?

Local youth hostel.

Then why drive, you could do it over the phone? Call the hostel, say you're with the English Tourist Board, ask about school parties. Do they get them at this time of year, what attracts them: you know the sort of thing. When they tell you there's one in at the moment, you ask where from.

Hmm. I *could* do it that way, DP, but I think I might get more if I'm actually there. Stuff on the brother himself, perhaps. You know: is he just like any other kid, or are there telltale signs? Is he a loner? How does he relate to girls in the group? Is it right that unsuspecting parents should send their daughters to share sleeping accommodation with the brother of a serial killer? With a bit of tweaking, we could work this up into the sort of womb-trembler that brings mobs out and sells papers. DP?

I'm still here, Minnie, and I think you're absolutely right. Get yourself up there. Observe. What's the supervision like? Are the kids chaperoned at all times? Is Dale Ward ever alone with females? Root out the *slightest* inadequacy and we'll implicate the teachers, the school, the local education authority: the *government*, why not? This one has the potential to make Willie Pegram's game look like something you'd find going on in a marquee at a Methodist garden fête. Go for it, sweetheart.

Thanks, DP.

63

Morning, Parish. Dennis Hawthorne sits down opposite me and smirks across the table. At three this morning, staggering to the lav, I'd caught him tiptoeing from the direction of the girls' wing. Neither of us had spoken, but the smirk was already in place. I thought I knew who he'd been with and it didn't help me sleep. Now, reaching for the cornflakes packet, he says, I don't know about you, Parish, but I'm shattered. Didn't shut my eyes till after three.

Yes you did, chirps Sally, two places down on my side. You shut them twice at least.

Carla Moffat lets out a mew, claps a hand to her mouth to keep from spraying cornflakes on the tablecloth. It's a deliberate wind-up, of course: he probably hadn't even *been* to the east wing. I go into *don't give a stuff* mode, sipping coffee and looking past Hawthorne's shoulder at the bright window.

We're outside by nine, knapsacks and all the kit. It's a sharp morning, frost on fallen leaves, trees skeletal against a blue sky. Shikey's chuffed. I'm glad we were rained off yesterday, he says, surveying the scene through a cloud of his own breath. Forecast's for snow flurries this evening, but we'll be back indoors by then, snug as a bug in a rug.

Snug as a bug in a rug. What a plonker. We set off in a ragged line, him leading, Emma bringing up the rear. Will

Tomlinson at my side goes, D'you know they once had a parson here who'd drive people into church with a whip?

Yes, I sigh, *and* I know about the coiners who dropped their idiot kid in a bog because he grassed 'em up, and the house they lived in's known as Drop Farm to this day. I know *all* the stories round here, Will.

Rude, I know: cruel even, but I had enough of his rabbit on the coach. Better the clomp of boots, rustle of waterproof coats, Shikey's occasional commentaries when we're passing places of interest. Or of little interest, depending on your point of view.

Our route hasn't taken us near Mrs Sugden's crossing, and that's good. No baying mob outside Langlands this morning either: perhaps the lollipop lady's decided to keep my presence to herself. If so I can stop worrying about her, and if I can shove Sally Prentice to the back of my mind as well, I might even squeeze a bit of enjoyment out of the day. This *is* my backyard after all, and there's no place like home.

We're on a lane called Cemetery Road. The land falls away on our right, there's a terrific view along the valley: fields, farms, a reservoir. On our left the moors begin, black and grey this time of year. Will says, I hope it's not roads all the way.

I shake my head. It's not; you'll see a track in front of us soon. We take that, and it gets rougher and steeper as we go along: a lot steeper than Hangingwood Down. Top Withens is just under the horizon to your right, but it blends in with the landscape: you can only see it when there's snow on the ground.

He pulls a face. No snow, thanks, it's cold enough already.

I grin. This isn't *cold*, you soft git. Do you good, six feet of snow: make a man of you.

Things're closing in on me from two directions even as I speak: *white* things. Good job I don't know.

64

Ah, good morning. Thought the bell wasn't working.

I was cleaning upstairs, I'm here on my own. How can I help you?

My name's Veronica Craven, I do research for the tourist board. I'd like to ask you a couple of questions if that's all right. Won't take long.

You'd better come in but I *am* rather busy: got a school party staying.

I promise I won't keep you, Mrs . . .?

Tinsley, Beth Tinsley. And it's Ms.

Sorry, one does tend to assume . . .

I know, happens all the time.

I'm sure. Oddly enough, it's school parties I'm interested in, Ms Tinsley, so you've already answered my first question: you *do* get school parties this time of year. Do these winter visitors tend to be fairly local, or might they come from just about anywhere?

Oh, pretty much anywhere. The one we've got now's come all the way from Devon.

Good heavens! Whereabouts in Devon, d'you know?

Yes, Market Flaxton. Their school's Market Flaxton High.

Market Flaxton High, fancy that. And where are they today, Ms Tinsley: the parsonage?

No, they did that yesterday. They're walking to Top Withens; should be there by now, eating packed lunches.

Brrrr! Rather them than me. Which other local attractions do school parties favour, would you say?

Well, the steam railway's a favourite. And there are various walks, though they're more popular in the summer months. It's the Brontës really, of course: the village itself, places round about with Brontë connections.

Hmm. And Top Withens is one of these?

Yes, some people say it was the model for Wuthering Heights.

How far is it from here?

About four miles.

Is it driveable?

No, it's moorland track. Look, this pamphlet tells you all about it; it's got a map. And now I really must get on, Ms Craven, if you'll excuse me.

Of course, you've been most helpful. Goodbye, Ms Tinsley, and thank you.

Gotcha!

65

We stop for a breather by the Brontë Waterfall. That's what it's called, but really it's just a thread of water that trickles down a rocky cleft. In summer it often dries up altogether and once, when they wanted a photo of it for a postcard, they dammed it at the top till water accumulated, then burst the dam and took the shot. It looks like Yorkshire's own Niagara, but it's a con.

The trickle empties into a stream that you cross on a little stone bridge, known to nobody's surprise as the Brontë Bridge. Beyond the bridge the terrain rises steeply, and it's uphill all the way to our destination. Some of the kids're appalled.

We going up there, sir? croaks Andy Burroughs.

We are, confirms Shikey.

Walking, sir?

Yes, lad, unless you fancy waiting for a bus. He looks at me. It's easier than it looks though, isn't it, Parish?

No, sir, it's harder. People've died up there in the wrong kit, it's deceptive.

Well, yes, in bad weather I dare say . . . no worries today though, eh? *Look* at it. He indicates the clear sky with a sweep of his hand. I shrug, hate being singled out. He gives up, goes and sits on a boulder with Emma, peels a banana.

Will's found a boulder as well. I join him on it and he

says, I read that Top Withens is nothing like *Wuthering Heights*.

I shake my head. It's not.

So why go?

Well, they reckon Emily used to walk past it, had its desolate setting in mind when she created *Wuthering Heights*. It's become part of the legend.

Hey, Glen an' Willie. Sally saunters over, mocking us with gorgeous eyes. Does my bum look big in these? She's wearing jeans, flared from the knee, tight everywhere else. Her bum doesn't look big, it looks fantastic and she knows it. I wish, *really* wish it left me cold, but she's not in a thong and I'm a hog for a pantie-line. I'm practically drooling, I hate myself.

Will's got more dignity. *Big?* he growls. Makes the Millennium Dome look like a zit, girl.

Millennium Dome. Where'd he *get* that, nerdy kid like him? All *I* can think to say is, He's right, Sally, I'd sit down if I were you.

She keeps the smile in place, but some of the kids've overheard and sniggered, and you can tell it's got to her. She flounces off, trying for cool, but her ears're red and I'd do anything for half an hour alone with her, red ears and all. No pride, that's my trouble.

Or is it?

All right, goes Shikey. He's finished whispering with Emma through mouthfuls of banana, stands up. This is where the going gets tough and the tough get going. You tough, Burroughs?

Tough enough, sir.

We'll see. He sticks his thumbs through the straps of his knapsack and leads us across the bridge like General Bradley. Me and Will bring up the rear, just in front of Emma.

Halfway up the first pitch, the column straggles to a halt because Shikey's stopped. He's pretending to study the little map on the pamphlet Beth gave him, but the truth is he led us off too fast and knackered himself. I can see his chest heaving from right back here.

Emma scowls up the hill. Why've we stopped?

I think Shi– . . . Mr Fenton's orienteering, Miss, says Will.

Rubbish, there's only the one track. *Resting*, that's what Mr Fenton's doing, Tomlinson.

Yes, Miss. Interesting, teachers undermining each other to pupils. Either she's not as gone on him as he is on her, or she's covering both sets of tracks.

Shikey takes two minutes to choose our route from the only one available, then he's climbing again. I'm turning to continue when I notice a fleck of blue against the winter drab below. Somebody's on the Brontë Bridge, looking up.

66

Minnie Cooper shades her eyes with a hand. *There he is, right at the back with his pal. Parish, the teacher called him, so that's the family name now.* She knows she has the right boy, for didn't the teacher consult him about the terrain, and didn't he answer in a local accent?

She can even see how they might have hit on the name. Local authorities split their territories into wards, the church divides its diocese into parishes. Ward. Parish. Clever in a way. *Wonder what he's changed Dale to?*

They're moving on, but the journalist waits on the bridge. Wouldn't do to look like she's shadowing them. All she needs to do is keep them in sight. So far there's just been the one minor lapse, when the teachers were busy chatting each other up and didn't notice the tarty-looking girl flaunting her charms in front of the psychopath's crazier brother. They've probably no idea who he is, but that's the whole point, isn't it – they *ought* to have.

The party's well ahead now; time for her to tackle the slope. The sun's up but there's not much warmth in it; she's wishing she'd worn something more suitable. Jeans are all right for driving or walking the dog and so's a showerproof jacket, but she's hardly equipped for the Yorkshire tops and she knows it. What did Ward/Parish say as she lurked shivering behind that rock? *People've died up there in the wrong kit.* Still, no use worrying now. Slog on, old chap, as Wilson said to Oates.

67

I must've done this trek at least a dozen times in my life, know practically every inch of it, but it seems further today than I remember. Must be the company. Last time I was up here was two and a half years ago, with Gav and a packet of tuna butties. And if somebody, MacBeth's three witches say, had told us that day that thirty months from now my brother'd be doing life and I'd be up here with a new name and a bunch of tossers from Devon, I'd've told 'em they were barmy. Gob-smacking how things change.

Talking of change, the sky's no longer clear. Not all over. There's dark cloud piling up on the western horizon, where most of our weather comes from. Cumulonimbus. Shikey doesn't seem to have noticed, even though he's just pointed out Top Withens and the cloud's right behind it. There's a bit of a breeze too, which wasn't there before. I think if I was the teacher, I'd be inclined to kick the picnic into touch and get everybody off the tops quick-sticks, but I'm not, so on we go.

Is this *it*? goes Wilson when we finally reach the ruined farmhouse.

It is, says Shikey, shrugging off his knapsack. You sound disappointed, lad.

It hasn't even got a roof, sir.

It's a *ruin*, boy, not a McDonald's.

I know, but I seen a picture of it with a roof.

Yes, well it wasn't *always* roofless, you fool. The picture shows Top Withens as it used to be, when it was a farm.

Well, I dunno why anyone'd want to do that climb we done, sir, just to gawp at some dump wivout a roof.

Wilson, you are totally devoid of that spiritual component which separates us from the rest of the animal kingdom. *What* are you totally devoid of?

Sir, that spiral computer wot suppurates . . .

Thank you, Wilson, that'll do. Shikey turns to the rest of us. Right, folks, this is it, have a good look. You're Emily Brontë, you've toiled up that track in heavy, restrictive clothing and narrow, thin-soled shoes. Your head's bursting with ideas for a novel, it needs a wild setting, here's Top Withens. What inspirations surge in your breast as you behold the isolated house: its stones blasted, its windows rattled by a thousand howling tempests? What thoughts of violent deeds and ghastly hauntings assail your sensitive soul when you gaze . . .

Sir?

Yes, Laura?

Is there a toilet?

68

There isn't a toilet, and the packed lunch is a bit yucky as well. A bully-beef and hard-boiled egg butty, packet of crisps, a fruit yoghurt and an apple. Just what you need after a hard climb in brass-monkey conditions.

Laura finds herself a quiet corner in the ruins while the rest of us sit around on stones and tussocks and tackle the rations. Nobody's done much looking except you-know-who, busy now between bites scribbling in his notebook. I'm at the yoghurt stage when a woman comes slogging up the track, dressed for shopping. Her silk scarf's the bit of blue I spotted a while back. She nods and smiles at Shikey and Emma, commences to view Top Withens from various angles, taking her time.

I'm watching the sky. Slowly but surely the cumulo-nimbus rears, rolls east across the blue, silently stalking the sun. The teachers're sitting on a fallen roof beam, up close, sharing a yoghurt. They're facing back the way we came, the threat behind them. I don't want to stick my nose in, like I'm telling them how to do their job, but we have what's called a Potentially Serious Situation here. I mean it might be nothing: the cloud might pass over, the forecast said snow flurries *tonight*. But forecasts can be wrong, and *flurries* isn't the word that springs to mind as I gaze at those looming mountains of vapour.

Sir?

What is it, Parish? He's peeved, I'm interrupting something.

I nod to the west. You might want to look at those clouds, sir, it could snow.

Huh? He twists round, so does Emma. Oh, yes, I see what you mean. Doesn't look too promising, does it? All right. He stands up. Listen, folks: looks as though we could be in for a spot of poor weather, so what I think we'll do is pack up, get into our kags and leggings and start back. He looks at Emma. Five minutes, Miss Royd?

Five minutes, Mr Fenton.

Thanks, Parish, he might add, but doesn't. I toss my apple to a sheep that's been watching me eat, cram the other stuff in my knapsack in place of my leggings and kagoul, start putting them on. The woman in the blue scarf completed her inspection of the ruins a few minutes ago and has moved on. She's out of sight round the shoulder of a hill. She'd only a dinky shoulder bag with her, no weather kit. I'd better mention it.

Miss?

Emma's tugging up a pair of green overtrousers. She looks up. Yes, Parish?

That woman, Miss, the one who came past. She'd nothing with her, no weather kit. D'you think we should . . .

Parish. Shikey's head appears through the neckhole of the kag he's pulling on. You might have been first to notice the cloud, lad, but don't get carried away. It's not your job to round up every Tom, Dick and Harry on the moor, just because you used to visit here. Get your stuff on and mind your own business.

Emma looks at me, shrugs ever so slightly. She'd've done something, I *know* she would, but Shikey's in charge. She can't very well argue with him in front of everybody, but if she knows what a prat he is, why does she let him cuddle up, share her yoghurt? I don't get adults, they're something else.

It takes a bit longer than five minutes, but we're all kitted up and on the track when the first snowflakes whirl.

69

Minnie Cooper stands where she can see without being seen. She's damned cold, but you don't get the best stories by sitting in cosy lounges with a glass in your hand. Those teachers're totally wrapped up in each other again, the pupils could be getting up to anything. The killer's more dangerous brother seems to be playing with that apple, rather than eating it. The kid beside him's obviously the school nerd, scribbling in a notebook where a normal boy'd be horsing around with his mates. It figures, two misfits together.

She's not sure which direction the party will take when they decide they've had enough of Top Withens, so she holds herself ready to stay out of their sight whichever way they go. As it turns out, her wait is not as long as it might have been. She watches as they wriggle into windproof clothing, wishing her own wasn't hanging in the utility room 200 miles away. When they move off, it's down the track they came up by. She's retracing her steps towards the ruins when it starts to snow.

What to do? If it's going to be just a shower, she might be as well taking shelter in the old building till it eases off: at least she'll be out of the wind. If it was going to go on snowing she'd need to get herself on to lower ground as quickly as possible, but it's not supposed to snow till tonight. She decides to take shelter and see what happens.

She stands in the angle of two stout walls and watches through a frameless window as the school party winds downhill like a drab green snake. The snow is falling more thickly: large feathery flakes whirling on gusts that boom about the house. She can hardly see the youngsters, the blizzard interposing itself like a fog. *This is no shower*, she tells herself. *I think I'd better follow while I can still see them.*

She abandons her shelter and hurries after them. By now they're visible only intermittently and the snow is starting to settle. It's over her shoes already and what's more frightening, it threatens to obliterate the track. The wind penetrates her inadequate clothing so easily she might as well be naked. As she stumbles downhill her foot finds a rolling pebble and goes from under her. She teeters, arms flailing, and sits down hard. At once, snow becomes icy water that passes through the seat of her jeans. When she gets to her feet she's soaked to the skin, there's no track and the party has disappeared.

70

It's coming thick and fast now, but we're doing all right. What you do is look for little humps in the snow. Over the years, walkers have dropped loose stones to form conical piles at intervals beside the track. It's sort of a casual tradition: pick up the odd stone, toss it on to the nearest pile, help some future traveller. The piles never get very high because lambs play King of the Castle on them, causing them to shift and slip, and children use them as ammo dumps, but they're high enough to act as mini-cairns in all but the heaviest snowfalls, keeping those who know what to look for on the right track. Shikey's a plonker, but he's obviously done some walking: he's using the cairns to good effect and we're making fair progress towards the valley.

I'm not happy though, can't get that woman out of my head. Dressed for shopping, lost on the tops in a snowstorm. It sounds melodramatic, but you can be dead in an hour up there. Only an idiot would set off in fashion kit in the middle of winter, but that doesn't mean she deserves to die.

At Gav's trial, his lawyer suggested that one of the victims, Virginia Mason, was practically asking to be attacked because of what she was wearing. Even *I* couldn't get my head round that and I was biased. Thinking about the poor woman we've just abandoned reminds me of Virginia Mason and it seems crazy now, but the idea forms in my mind of them as one and the same person. I can't explain, but that's what makes me do what I do next.

I have to go back for her. I'm not superstitious, never have been, but it feels like I'm being offered a chance here: I don't know what sort of chance. To make amends? No. Nothing can do that, ever. A chance though, of some sort. And I know I have to grab it, even if I die.

Giving Emma the slip's the easy bit. I go down on one knee, fiddling with an ice-clotted bootlace, and she strides past saying, Get a grip, Parish, we're not down yet. She doesn't wait for me though, and in ten seconds has merged with the whirling snow. I turn to face the wind.

I'm going outside: I may be some time.

71

I'm going to die. She stands ankle-deep, daren't move as the wind skims off heat, fledges her face and hands with snow-feathers and moulds thin, wet fabric like a clammy shroud to her body. *I was doing my job, that's all, and I'm going to die for it.* As a fresh young reporter she'd sometimes fantasized about losing her life on the job, caught up in crossfire perhaps, or stepping on a mine in some war-zone far from home. The prospect of such an end had seemed to her glorious: her personal heroines were war correspondents, most of them dead.

But, God, not like this. Going boldly into some front-line hot spot, intent on capturing the very flavour and essence of hand-to-hand combat is one thing: dying miserably of hypothermia because your boss is intent on hounding the unfortunate relatives of a murderer, and because you were too stupid to dress for the job is quite another.

Please, not like this.

72

And I find her. Not because I'm brilliant, but because I follow the little bumps and there she stands, halfway between two of them, with her back to me.

Hello? She doesn't hear because of the wind. I go up to her, touch her sleeve. She spins round, puts both hands to her mouth, backs away. The haunted eyes, fluttering scarf and wild, ice-clotted hair make her look like Cathy's ghost. We can't stay here, I shout. You'll freeze; got to find shelter quick.

Stay away from me, she cries. I know why you've come back; I've got a pistol in my bag.

Those are her exact words. I blink snowflakes off my lashes, shake my head. You don't need a pistol, not for me. I'll get us under cover.

No. She backs up again, shoe-tops briefly visible. She must be frozen. I'm not stupid, I know who you are.

I'm Glen Parish, I know these moors. Top Withens is nearest, there's a bothy.

I'm not one of your feather-headed disco chicks. My colleagues know where I am. If anything happens to me they'll know who's responsible.

If anything happens to you the *cold*'ll be responsible. And it's not *if*, it's *when*.

Get out of my way, she cries, I'm going down; my car's there.

I shake my head. You'll be a goner before you get halfway, state you're in. Anyway, I'm off to that bothy, you can come with me or stay here and freeze, whichever. I step round her and go on, half blinded by the blizzard. I'm deadly cold, which means hypothermia's close. The woman must be on the verge of collapse, but I can't force her to come: can't *carry* her. And I'm damned if I'm going to stand there arguing till we both drop.

She follows. After a few paces I glance back and there she is, using my footholes like the page in 'Good King Wenceslas'. I don't like her: *I know who you are* means she's probably press, which means if she's alive tomorrow my cover's blown and we'll have to run away again, but all the same I don't want her to die. I wait, and when she catches up I circle her waist with my arm and help her go a bit faster. She's not happy about it, but she's too scared, too far gone to resist.

We toil on up. I'm following cairns, but it seems a heck of a long way to Top Withens. I'm half convinced we've passed it somehow when the ruins finally material-ize through the white-out and I half push, half drag my fainting companion to the bothy door.

The bothy's a lean-to stuck on the end of the ruin. The Countryside Service has roofed it and fitted a door so they can store tools and stuff inside. It's padlocked to keep visitors out, but padlocks can be broken if necessary and it's necessary now. I prop the woman against the lintel and give her a shake.

Your pistol.

Huhh . . .? She's semi-conscious.

Your pistol, to shoot the lock.

No. She shakes her ice-tatty head. No . . . pistol.

I never thought there was. Wait here then. As soon as I let go she subsides into a crumpled heap on the step, but I can't help that. I hurry along the house front and through a doorway into what was once a room. Debris is strewn across the earthen floor, covered mostly now by a scum of snow. I'm looking for something made of iron, something I can use as a lever, and it must be my lucky day, because propped against the wall in a corner is a two-foot length of rusty bar, hammered flat at both ends for screw holes.

She's still in a heap, not moving. My fingers are stiff, half numb, but I get one end of the bar through the hasp and spring the padlock with a fierce downward jerk.

It's dark inside: the bothy has no window. There's stuff everywhere; I collide with things at every step. Working blind, I clear a gritty bit of floor space and drag the woman inside. She's just about conscious and lies on her back, groaning and muttering. It's probably cold in here, but we're out of the wind, which makes it seem warm. I half close the door, I need a bit of light, and open my knapsack. Folded at the bottom is something I've carried all my life and never had to use. It's a man-size bag made of heavy-duty polythene. How you use it is, you get inside, pull it right up to your chin and lie still. The bag's seamless, no wind can get in, no body heat can escape. It's not comfy like a quilted sleeping bag, but it'll keep hypothermia at bay, even under the stars. All I have to do now is get my companion inside it.

And myself.

73

It's harder than you think, packing a limp adult into a polythene bag. It's probably easier if she's kicking and wriggling: you can use some of her own movement against her, or I suppose you can; I've never actually tried. Anyway, I get her in eventually, and the effort's brought my circulation back. It seems to have done a bit for her as well, her eyes are open and she's trying to lift her head, which gives me the opportunity to start getting the scarf from round her neck.

What're you *doing*? She clutches the thing with both hands. I thought she was too out of it to notice.

Let go, I need it: it shows at a distance.

She holds on though. I have to really tug, and even then I only get it because it's slippery, it slides through her grip. As I snatch it clear she cries out, and it's then I realize what's up. She thinks I mean to strangle her with it 'cause that was Gavin's thing.

She's whimpering, curling away from me. I shake my head. No! It's for a marker, to show 'em where we are. It's a good strong colour, I saw it half a mile away. I try to reassure her but I don't think she's taking it in: cold and exhaustion've fuddled her brain. I stand up, cross to the door.

The wind's terrific and there's nothing on the bothy to secure the scarf. I put it on top of the house wall, under a block of millstone grit. It snaps and flutters, a metre of brilliant blue. A searcher'd have to be blind, and even then he'd probably *hear* it.

The woman's conscious all right: it becomes obvious as soon as I try to join her in the bag. She's got the top all bunched up in her hands, she pulls it away from me, rolls on to her side to trap it under her.

Come *on*, Miss, I plead. I don't mean you any harm, I need to get warm, that's all.

No! she shakes her head. Stay away from me, just stay away.

But I'm wet through, *look*. D'you want me to die? I'll die if I can't get warm.

There's more, a *lot* more, before she relents or comes to her senses or whatever and lets me crawl in with her. It's a tight flipping fit I can tell you, but *warm*? It's like being teleported straight from Top Withens to Kingston, Jamaica. I don't cuddle up to her so don't think it. I don't even *like* her, and you can bet she doesn't like me. Involuntary contact is what it is, back to back, soaking up each other's warmth till we stop shivering and start drifting away. It's excruciating to lie on a cement floor, especially when you're shrink-wrapped, but we sleep anyway.

And when we wake up we're different.

74

The scarf works. It's still only half-light when the door scrapes open and a guy with a lamp on his head growls, Fell Rescue: you two OK? He doesn't sound surprised, so maybe he finds people bagged up in pairs all the time.

We're fine, goes my companion. I think she's been awake a while: she's getting up. I'm still at the grunting stage and the light's making my eyes water.

Yeah, I manage. Thanks for coming.

'S all right, he says. We'd a fair idea where you'd be. He nods at the poly bag. You did everything right, including the lady's scarf. Hang on while I call in.

He talks into a mobile while I'm folding the bag. I'm stiff as hell and the cold's seeping through my damp kit, but those aren't my chief worries. Now the danger's past it starts to hit me what'll happen today. My bedfellow's a tabloid hack, eager to tell the great British public what the Ward family's calling itself nowadays and where it lives. The fact that we've slept together'll cut no ice at all, no joke intended. I must call home, prepare the family for another blitz of sanctimonious headlines.

It's amazing: they won't let us walk. Fifteen minutes after the call-in the place is crawling with guys and girls in yellow hard hats, carrying stretchers and moon blankets. We protest, but it's no use: we're stretchered out of the bothy and into a Land Rover, which bumps and bounces us down from the tops and then by way of snow-ploughed roads to hospital.

We lie on trolleys in adjoining cubicles. A doctor comes. He checks the hack first; I hear her through the curtain whispering to him, probably asking for her phone so she can call in her rotten scoop. He tells her she must lie quietly, her temperature's still on the low side.

He looks in on me. I say I'm here under false pretences, taking up a desperately needed bed. It isn't a bed, he says, only a trolley. And there are no false pretences, I'm told you're a hero.

I shake my head. No, I'm not.

He smiles. Two gentlemen in reception think you are: they're waiting to interview you, take your picture.

No! I say it louder than I mean to, but isn't this the *last* thing I need?

The doctor shrugs. They're from the local rag, it's a weekly; you'll be back in Devon before it's out. I'm afraid I told them it'd be all right as long as they don't . . .

Doctor. My late bedfellow sticks her face round the curtain. She's got a card in her hand, flaps it at him. I'm Minnie Cooper of the *Post*, and we've signed this kid to a world exclusive. You tell those local guys that if they take *one* picture or print a *single* word, my boss Danvers Pilkington'll be down on their editor like a mad rhinoceros. *And* he'll sue this hospital for facilitating a breach of contract. Be sure to tell 'em it's *Danvers Pilkington* they're screwing around with: they'll recognize the name.

The doctor, poor guy, goes off to deliver the message. I look at the woman. Minnie Cooper?

That's right.

Do you drive a white Polo?

Yes, I do.

On the Isle of Wight?

One time, yes.

You followed my mother.

Did I?

You know you did. Anna Ward.

Ward? She frowns. I thought you said she was your mother.

She is.

But your name's Parish, isn't it?

You know very well who I am. The lollipop lady told you I was here, that's why you came. I look her in the eye. You haven't signed me to any exclusive though, and you won't, no matter who your rotten boss is.

She shakes her head. I'm afraid you're still confused, Glen: hypothermia'll do that. All this stuff about wards and lollipop ladies and rotten bosses, it's nonsense. She comes right into my cubicle, sits on the edge of the trolley. What game's she playing?

She says, all I know is you're Glen Parish, a schoolboy from Devon who saved my life last night. I don't know any lollipop ladies, or anybody called Ward, and as for the rotten boss you mentioned, well, who needs that sort of boss, eh?

She bends suddenly, kisses me on the forehead. Thanks, Glen, she murmurs, for saving my life in more ways than one. She stands up, winks at me and disappears through the curtain.

DP, it's Minnie.

Oh, hi, Minnie. Don't tell me – you've flushed 'em out at last, right?

No, DP, it's not about that.

It *isn't*? Well, you better tell me what it *is* about, young woman, because I don't mind telling you I'm getting mightily hacked off waiting for things to resolve here.

It's about me telling you where you can stick your job, DP.

Huh, *what*'s that you say? You're breaking up, Minnie.

No, I'm *not*, DP. I've never been so together in my life, which is why I'm telling you what you can do with your lousy job.

Are you *crazy*? Nobody talks that way to Danvers Pilkington. You'll never work in journalism again.

That's right, DP, never again, and d'you know how that makes me feel: *clean*. I feel clean.

Go to hell, Cooper.

Save me a seat, DP.

I don't see her again. She discharges herself, and an hour later they let me go too. No trace of the local press, just Shikey with a taxi. He gives me a bollocking for causing Emma and himself a sleepless night, then tells me what I did was wonderful. There was a reporter, he says, and a photographer. They were waiting to make you famous, then a doctor came and whispered something and they rushed off. Shame.

Shame my foot. I'm not the only one who's glad it won't be in the papers: they'd have crucified him for not supervising the group properly. He knows it too, but he doesn't know I know: I'm just a kid.

The rest of the week is as uneventful as only a week in Haworth can be. We gawp at Brontë stuff in the area: houses, ruins, graves. It's nearly as exciting as Will's dolmens, I don't know how I stand it. But the thing is – and this *is* the thing – I feel terrific all the time, as if I'm walking on air. I don't mind that it's just another heap of mossy old stones: I'm happy knowing I'm the same as everybody else. My feelings are normal feelings, even when I'm letching after Sally Prentice. Rolf tried to tell me months ago, but I couldn't believe him. Now I can, ever since I woke up in that bothy with Minnie Cooper and she was all right.

We leave Friday and it's good to be home. I do brilliant

in Shikey's *Wuthering Heights* test, though I say it myself. I come top, beating Will Tomlinson for the first and only time. And I don't even get stuffed into a wheelie bin for being a swot.

It's not all fun though. Christmas Eve, a country-and-western song comes on the radio. It's about Christmas in prison, the guy's writing home:

> *It's Christmas in prison, there'll be music tonight*
> *I'll prob'ly get homesick, I love you, good night.*

When this reaches Mum's brain she drops the batch of mince pies she's just slid from the oven and runs howling out of the kitchen. Scares Kayleigh half to death. Just a mushy song, but it replays in my skull all next day, and I know Mum and Dad hear it too.

Mostly though, things are getting better. I'm not being Glen Parish any more, I *am* Glen Parish. Nobody's looking for us. Rolf says there's a sad bit in everybody's life: it's part of the deal. Gav's our sad bit, I suppose, but when I picture him I see him happy that *I'm* happy, on a long-lost August day at Flamingoland.

hotnews@puffin

Hot off the press!
You'll find all the latest exclusive Puffin news here

Where's it happening?
Check out our author tours and events programme

Bestsellers
What's hot and what's not? Find out in our charts

E-mail updates
Sign up to receive all the latest news
straight to your e-mail box

Links to the coolest sites
Get connected to all the best author web sites

Book of the Month
Check out our recommended reads

www.puffin.co.uk